"What are you s

She had been trying not to think beyond tonight, or let herself feel anything that wasn't in the moment. Now Liam was ruining the mood by talking about the future consequences.

Liam cleared his throat. "A fling."

"Excuse me?" For a moment, Mae thought she'd misheard him.

"I don't see why we should deny ourselves some fun. But, I also know we're both still hurting from our last relationships. I thought perhaps, if you agree, we could keep things casual. You know, see each other in private."

Liam ducked his head with a grin, almost bashful. It was nice to see that perhaps he wasn't as confident as he often portrayed. She liked seeing that softer side of him. It represented him opening up, letting that brash exterior slip so she could see a more vulnerable Liam. The one who didn't want to risk getting hurt again either.

"I just know we would have a really good time together." He pulled her close, capturing the gasp of surprise on her lips with his. The kissing alone was sufficient to prove his point.

Dear Reader,

When I was asked to write a book around St. Patrick's Day, my mind went immediately to the parade. They're such a spectacle all around the world I knew I could have some fun celebrating all things Irish!

In the manner of those stereotypical romcoms based in Ireland, I thought I'd throw in a wisecracking Irishman and an American seemingly impervious to his charms. Of course that's never the case…

Beneath the surface, Liam is hiding a broken heart and doing his best to raise his daughter alone. Mae, who was jilted at the altar, has moved to Dublin to start a new life—one that doesn't include any significant other with the potential to abandon her. She has locked herself away from the world in order to protect her fragile heart.

So, when she finds herself inextricably linked with Liam through an inebriated St. Patrick, and his enormous Irish wolfhound, her life is turned upside down.

I hope you enjoy every leprechaun and shamrock I've thrown at this book celebrating Ireland, the people and the culture. It's a magical place that deserves to be shared with everyone.

Happy reading!

Love,

Karin x

AN AMERICAN DOCTOR IN IRELAND

———

KARIN BAINE

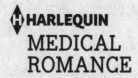

HARLEQUIN
MEDICAL
ROMANCE

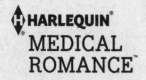

HARLEQUIN®
MEDICAL ROMANCE™

Recycling programs for this product may not exist in your area.

ISBN-13: 978-1-335-59531-7

An American Doctor in Ireland

Copyright © 2024 by Karin Baine

For questions and comments about the quality of this book, please contact us at CustomerService@Harlequin.com.

Harlequin Enterprises ULC
22 Adelaide St. West, 41st Floor
Toronto, Ontario M5H 4E3, Canada
www.Harlequin.com

Printed in U.S.A.

Karin Baine lives in Northern Ireland with her husband, two sons and her out-of-control notebook collection. Her mother and her grandmother's vast collection of books inspired her love of reading and her dream of becoming a Harlequin author. Now she can tell people she has a *proper* job! You can follow Karin on Twitter @karinbaine1 or visit her website for the latest news, karinbaine.com.

Books by Karin Baine

Harlequin Medical Romance

Carey Cove Midwives

Festive Fling to Forever

Royal Docs

Surgeon Prince's Fake Fiancée
A Mother for His Little Princess

A GP to Steal His Heart
Single Dad for the Heart Doctor
Falling Again for the Surgeon
Nurse's Risk with the Rebel

Harlequin Romance

Pregnant Princess at the Altar

Visit the Author Profile page
at Harlequin.com for more titles.

For me, because I don't give myself
nearly enough credit! x

CHAPTER ONE

A SEA OF green spread out before Mae Watters. Well, it was a crowd of people dressed for St Patrick's Day. They didn't dye the River Liffey in Dublin green especially for the occasion, the way they did back home in Boston, but it still reminded her of every seventeenth of March she'd spent with her mother at the parade there. And, when she was old enough, they'd graduated to the Irish-themed pubs to celebrate the day.

A year without her had been difficult. Not least because Mae had had no one to turn to when, humiliatingly, her relationship had come to an end. Being jilted at the altar eight months ago, and being left alone in Ireland to pick up the pieces left of her heart, had left her feeling more alone than ever.

It wasn't as though she had any family left in America to go back to—at least, none who wanted to know her. The father who'd left her when she was little could have started a new family and given her half-brothers and sisters, but she'd never know, as he'd disappeared completely out of her life.

'Excuse us.' A family dressed as leprechauns squeezed past her on the footpath, keen to get to the best vantage point for the parade. She envied the young couple pushing the double stroller transporting a baby and toddler, giddy with excitement. Not because she wanted children, or even a husband now, but because of the family unit it represented—something she'd never have. She'd lost too much, too many loved ones, ever to open herself up to anyone again and to have a chance of starting a family of her own.

Perhaps she shouldn't have come here today, when her spirits weren't as high as everyone else's. Music was blasting all along the street and people were singing, clapping and waving Irish flags as the floats came past to celebrate the patron saint of Ireland. All she wanted to do was cry. But it was a rare day off before she started her new job, it was her Mum's home city and she'd thought she'd feel closer to her here. The problem was, she had, until she remembered that the cruelty of illness had separated them for ever. It was a cruel irony to specialise in medicine when you couldn't save your own mother.

'Ye—oh!'

She was jostled off-balance by a man carrying a little girl high on his shoulders as they pushed in beside her, dancing to the music. Usually, common sense would have prevented her from confronting a tattooed male with bright-green hair, but today her emotions were all over the place.

'Do you mind?' She bristled, rubbing her elbow, which had been banged in the melee.

'Not at all, love!' He grinned, the twinkling blue eyes and bright-white smile not intimidating in the slightest.

Perhaps that was why she wouldn't drop the issue.

'Well, I do mind. I was standing minding

my own business until you rudely pushed past me.'

'Sorry, missus. The wee one wanted to see,' he said without a hint of genuine remorse.

'You should pinch her, Dad.'

'Excuse me?'

'It's a tradition. You're supposed to wear green today to remain invisible to the leprechauns, otherwise you get pinched.'

Despite the man's explanation of why his daughter was so keen for him to assault her, Mae wasn't impressed by his behaviour.

'Perhaps you'd be better teaching her something about manners… And it's *Ms*, actually.' She didn't need the reminder that she hadn't actually got to the part where she'd changed her name, or even got a husband.

'Says it all,' he muttered.

Mae could feel her blood starting to boil at the utter gall of the man insulting her when he was the one in the wrong. If not for the presence of the child, she would've had a few choice words to say to him.

'What does?'

'Well, it's that time of the year, isn't it?

When all you Yanks come over thinking you'll bag an Irish husband.'

'How dare you?' she blustered. 'I live here.'

His rude comments made her bypass her usual polite manner when dealing with irascible men, common in her line of work, in which she'd learned to smile and plough on rather than react.

But today she rose to the bait. Probably because she'd finally reached her limit of things she could stand in this wet, miserable country. She had followed her heart here, hoping for the romantic fantasy of living happily ever after with her charming Irish fiancé in the seaside town of Bray, but she'd earned her place with every tear she'd shed since.

Especially when she'd been working to help the inhabitants of this country every day, despite her heartbreak. She'd moved out of the house she'd shared with Diarmuid, of course, but seeing him around the hospital had been too painful a reminder of what he'd done to her. Hopefully her move to the city would help her get over it.

The man took his eyes off the spectacle out

on the street to study her. 'Hmm. Then I'd wager you came back to find your Irish roots.'

Mae could feel the heat rising in her body, surely manifesting itself in those tell-tale red splotches that oft appeared on her neck when she was riled, as though the effort of trying to hold her temper threatened to burst right through her skin.

'My mother came from Dublin.' She tried to keep the hysteria from her voice as she attempted to justify her residence in the city.

'Of course she did.'

Mae was getting used to the dry Irish sense of humour, the gentle teasing that came with a nudge in the ribs and a twinkle in the eye. However, there was something about this know-it-all stranger that was really pushing her buttons today and making her want to scream.

She hated the fact that her life had boiled down to that of stereotypical American in Ireland. It said nothing of the heartache and loss she'd gone through to get here. If she was this touchy over a few teasing comments now, it was probably for the best that she went home, before the crowd really started celebrating the day, leaving her even more of an outsider.

It occurred to her that she wasn't beholden to be polite to this man or stand anywhere near him. Arguing back wasn't going to achieve anything other than upsetting her, when she was thinking about her mum. And, if that smile on his face grew any wider, she'd be tempted to smack it off.

In an attempt to avoid a possible assault charge, or an emotional breakdown in front of the most annoying man on earth, she simply turned and walked away.

'Wait. I'm sorry.' Liam had seen the flash of pain in the redhead's jade-green eyes before she turned away.

He hadn't meant to upset her. His big mouth was always getting him into trouble. Today was supposed to be fun for everyone involved and he didn't want to be responsible for spoiling anyone's day. Sometimes his brand of humour didn't translate well with American visitors, earning him a clip around the ear from his mother even at the age of thirty-two, lest he offended any of her customers at the family pub. Which, today, should be welcoming as many tourists as possible.

Although he was first and foremost an A&E doctor in Dublin City Hospital, he was often roped in to collect empty glasses during busy periods in the pub. He and Shannon, his daughter, spent a lot of time there. Not because he was a drinker, but because his parents lived in the flat above the premises, and babysat when he was at work.

Since his partner of nine years, Clodagh, had left him—for his best friend, no less— he'd had to rely on help with the school run and occasionally in the evenings when he was working. Shifts in A&E weren't compatible with the life of a single dad. It wasn't the happy family life he'd planned, or the life he now wanted, and he was burdened with the guilt he'd let down his daughter, as well as asking too much of his parents for the best part of a year. The last thing he needed on his conscience was knowing he'd caused unnecessary upset to someone else.

Liam watched the blaze of red hair bobbing

through the crowd, a beacon in the green tide that made her easily identifiable.

'Da-ad! I can't see the parade,' Shannon complained as he followed the American away from the prime view he'd gone to so much trouble to secure.

'I know, sweetheart. I just need to speak to the lady again.'

'The pretty lady with the red hair?' Shannon kicked her heels into his chest to indicate she wanted to dismount his shoulders. Liam bent down as far as he could, reached up and lifted her down on to the ground. She took off before he could even ask what she was up to.

'Shannon! Don't run away!' he shouted, to no avail, and was forced to chase after the green tutu disappearing into the crowd. In pursuit of his daughter, he dodged mums with prams and men with cans in their hands, his heart pounding with the fear of losing her in the crowd. Although she knew the city well, she was only seven years old. She was his baby. She was all he had. He caught sight of her as she located the American redhead, though she remained out of his reach.

Shannon tugged on the belt of the woman's white wool coat. 'My dad wants to speak to you. I can't see the parade until you talk to him.'

Unfortunately, his offspring had inherited his lack of tact, leaving him cringing as the woman watched him approach.

'I'm so sorry. Both for my daughter accosting you, and for upsetting you earlier. I was joking about the whole "Irish roots" thing.' He took Shannon's hand and discreetly pulled her to his side.

The redhead arched an eyebrow at him. 'No, you weren't. You were enjoying belittling me. Believe it or not, a high percentage of Americans *are* actually of Irish origin. My mother was a Dublin girl. I moved here last year after she died. So, in future please think before you judge people.'

'I apologise for thinking I was being funny.'

'You're not,' the American and his daughter chorused.

'Apparently…' He tucked that little nugget

away for future reference, something to add to his list of failures.

'Do you often use your daughter to get women to talk to you?' Red asked, clearly enjoying watching him squirm.

It was the price he'd have to pay for sticking his size tens in it in the first place.

'Not often, no. Again, I can only apologise. If you're ever in O'Conner's in Westmoreland Street, I'll even buy you a pint to say sorry.'

'O'Conner's?'

'My parents own it—and you won't pay Temple Bar prices there.'

'I thought you were buying,' she said, quick as a flash.

'Only the first round. The next one's on you.' Were they flirting? He was so long out of the game, he couldn't tell. Though he wasn't interested in any Paddy's Day shenanigans, unlike most of the Irish population, he was enjoying the back and forth between them.

'Dad! Dad! There's Ray!'

Before he could get a definitive answer as to whether or not he'd see his new banter partner again, Shannon was tugging on his shirt and pointing towards the parade. Ray, their next-door neighbour, was walking head and shoulders above the rest of the parade. Easily done when he was wearing stilts, dressed as St Patrick in emerald-green robes, wore a mitre on his head, and carried a staff in his hand, chasing several people dressed as snakes.

'A friend of yours?' the American beauty asked as they watched his antics.

'Ray Jackson. My next-door neighbour.' Despite everyone else's enthusiasm, Liam couldn't quite bring himself to join in on the cheering.

'What's wrong? Did he steal your outfit?'

'No. He has an alcohol problem, and it looks very much to me as though he's been drinking already today.' Not a good idea to be drunk in charge of stilts, he was sure.

Right on cue, there was a collective gasp from the crowd as St Patrick began to topple, almost crushing one of the green leotard-clad snakes in the process.

'Can you keep an eye on Shannon for me?'

He didn't intend letting his daughter out of his sight, even if he had left her with a trustworthy-looking stranger, but being a doctor wasn't a job that finished at five o'clock, or even stopped on a day off.

'But I…'

With a patient and friend to attend to, he didn't wait around to hear the excuse.

'What are you playing at, Raymondo?' he asked, running over to assess the damage. The music and laughter had ceased now, happy faces etched with concern, fingernails being bitten as St Patrick lay in a heap in the middle of the road.

'I think I lost my balance. I'm getting too old for this.' Ray groaned through gritted teeth.

'You don't say. I'm going to have to take these things off you so I can get a proper look at that leg.' The right leg, which was crumpled under the middle-aged saint, looked to be at an odd angle. Liam gingerly began to undo the stilts fastened around his feet.

'Stop! Don't move him,' a now familiar American twang instructed.

'Can you stay back, please? I've got this. And where is my daughter?' Now that the redhead was walking towards him minus her charge, nausea began to swell in his stomach. He should never have taken his eyes off her.

'She's with her grandmother. Now, please move aside so I can take a look.' She knelt down beside him, regardless that her white coat would be covered in green glitter and paint from the road when she got up again.

At least Shannon was okay, and he was glad his mum had found time for a break after all—just in time for another spot of babysitting. He glanced over and gave her a thumbs-up when he spotted her hovering at the edge of the crowd. She gestured that she'd take Shannon back with her to the pub, leaving him to focus on the job at hand.

'Thanks, but I've got this,' he insisted. 'I'm a doctor.'

'So am I,' she countered, bringing them to a stalemate.

'Good for you.' He was surprised that an American doctor should have chosen to move to Ireland to work. This wasn't about egos;

Raymond was hurt and currently holding up the entire St Patrick's Day parade.

He could feel her bristle beside him. 'You don't look much like a doctor.'

'What happened to not being too judgemental? The green hair was "fun dad" showing up for Shannon today. It's my day off.'

'And the tattoos?'

He was tempted to tell her they were the marks of a misspent youth. It wasn't against the medical oath, or any of her business, how he'd chosen to adorn his body. However, it gave him huge satisfaction, seeing her face when he licked his thumb and smudged the Irish flag he'd drawn on his arm this morning to match the shamrocks he'd painted on Shannon's cheeks.

'Listen, I'm glad I have two doctors fighting over me—but no offence, Liam, I'd prefer the redhead.'

'Not appropriate, Ray,' Liam admonished as he rolled up the man's trouser leg to uncover a nasty open fracture. The broken bone was sticking up through the wound, the swelling around the area already apparent. Given the fact Ray wasn't writhing in agony, he suspected the alcohol he'd consumed had gone some way to dulling the pain—small mercies.

'I suppose this will get done quicker if we work together. Dr Mae Watters.' She held out her hand for him to shake, which he duly did.

'Dr Liam O'Conner. First things first, we need to call an ambulance.' He knew there were probably medical staff on hand to cover the parade, but Ray was going to need to be transferred to the hospital for treatment.

'I've done that, and we know he's conscious and responsive, if a tad inebriated.'

'Hey! I—I needed some Irish courage,' Ray hiccupped, the stench of booze and stale cigarettes making Liam and Mae recoil.

'We'll have to stabilise that leg.' It was necessary to immobilise the limb to prevent further injury until he reached hospital. Without a sterile dressing to hand, Liam used the green silk stole around Ray's neck to apply pressure to the wound without covering the bone.

'You can use my belt to fashion something

with the stilt,' Mae suggested, whipping out the tie from the waistband of her coat.

'Just let us know if it hurts or you start to feel nauseous, Ray. The paramedics will be able to give you something for the pain when they get here,' Mae reassured him as Liam worked quickly to bind the leg to the makeshift splint above and below the fracture, careful not to jar the leg any more than necessary.

'Ah, the good stuff...' Ray trailed off and Liam wondered exactly how much he had drunk this morning. He knew he wouldn't be honest with him about his alcohol consumption—he never was—though Liam heard the rattle of bottles going into the recycling bin every morning. It wouldn't be a good idea to mix painkillers with a skinful of alcohol, and he'd be sure to fill the ambulance crew in on his neighbour's history. At least, what he knew of it, from the drunken ramblings and numerous falls Ray had suffered since his partner had died a couple of years ago.

'We're going to be having another talk about your drinking, Ray.'

Ray batted away his concerns with a tut and an eyeroll. They'd both had their personal problems, but Ray had been a visible warning to Liam not to give into the self-pity which had descended upon him too when Clodagh left him just over a year ago. He hadn't wanted to become another shell of a man who could barely function. Shannon needed more from him than ever. She was the reason he got up every morning, and the reason he didn't drown his sorrows in the bottom of a glass every evening. He felt sorry for his neighbour; he saw the pity in Mae's eyes, and he never wanted anyone to look at him the same way.

As much as he might need to blot out the memory of Clodagh cheating on him, ending their relationship and walking out on their family, it would be selfish to do so. Even more than pretending his relationship hadn't been in trouble, because that would've meant admitting his failure as a partner and father. A fact which was public knowledge anyway, now that they were separated.

In hindsight, having a family had always

been his idea of an idyll, not Clodagh's. They had only been dating a few months when she'd fallen pregnant, before they'd even talked about whether or not they wanted marriage and children. It later became apparent that, unlike him, she hadn't wanted either. Whilst he'd been over the moon at the prospect of becoming a parent, she hadn't been as enthusiastic.

Still in her twenties, Clodagh had always given the impression she resented being tied down to the responsibility of having a child. Liam had done his best to carry most of the load, doing most of the childcare, giving her the freedom to still go out with her friends. Perhaps somewhere along the way he'd pushed her out, creating a strong bond with Shannon that mother and daughter had never quite mirrored. Liam had no doubt she loved Shannon, but even now she seemed an afterthought next to Clodagh's work and personal life. He wished he could forget about Clodagh, and her betrayal, just as easily.

When the sirens sounded, the crowd began to part so the ambulance could get through.

'Yeah, yeah. If you tell me you haven't been tempted to lose yourself in a bottle since Clodagh left you, then you're a liar,' Ray rambled.

Though Mae didn't comment, Liam could feel her eyes on him. He refused to look up and see that same pity in her eyes for him.

'I've been tempted, Ray, yes. But it doesn't solve anything, does it? Only makes things worse.' Liam was relieved when the ambulance arrived so they could stop discussing his failed relationship under the watchful gaze of the entire city. There was one pair of green eyes in particular before which he didn't want to appear weak. Not when he'd already made such a sterling impression on his new American friend... Despite her being the first woman he'd felt the urge to engage in conversation since Clodagh had left, now he'd be glad to climb into the ambulance and leave her behind.

He relayed Ray's current condition to the medics and waited as they transferred him into the back of the ambulance.

'Who's coming with him?'

'I am,' both Liam and Mae chorused.

'Which hospital are you taking him to?' he enquired, hoping the geography would give Mae a reason to back off.

'Dublin City.'

'That's where I work.' He played his trump card with a flourish.

'Me too.' Mae killed his sense of triumph dead before he'd even had the chance to blow his horn.

Though she looked surprised by the co-incidence, there was no sign of her backing down. If anything, she looked smug that she had as much right to accompany the patient as he did.

If this feisty American was going to be his new colleague, work was about to get a lot more interesting.

CHAPTER TWO

LIAM WAS ABLE to fast-track Ray through the Accident and Emergency department thanks to his position and a large dose of charm. Mae followed, keen to see the patient through, regardless of her male counterpart seeming to have things under control—or perhaps in spite of. She hated to think of him having the upper hand and getting rid of her so easily. Yes, it was his neighbour, but they'd both been on scene and, since this was her new place of work, she'd just as much right to be here as Dr O'Conner.

It felt weird to call him that. Yes, she'd been unfairly judgemental about his appearance, but his demeanour around her thus far had left a lot to be desired. Even if he had worked well in a medical crisis.

'You can go home, if you want. I'll stay and make sure Ray is comfortable,' Liam told her outside the cubicle.

'I'd rather be here. I don't like his colour, and if you're right about his drinking…. I noticed distention of his abdomen, which could be due to the release of fluid from his liver, and the swelling in his lower legs might be fluid retention.' She was familiar with the yellowing complexion in long-term alcohol abusers and what it meant. All the symptoms she had noticed were indicative of liver disease—not things which would clear up of their own accord, and certainly not if the patient continued to drink heavily.

'I've thought the same thing myself for a long time but it's been next to impossible getting him to go to the doctor. That's why I've ordered a battery of tests while he's here, the full MOT, so I can be fully prepared when I go into battle and try to talk to him about his drinking problem again.'

Okay, so when he wasn't teasing and making rude, stereotypical jokes at her expense, he did sound like a doctor, and a good neighbour. It was one thing to strap up a broken leg and get someone to the hospital, but quite another to order up extra blood tests and wait for the results, on a hunch. Especially when it was his day off and he had a daughter at home.

Mae had heard the snippet of information about his personal life revealed by his inebriated friend and she couldn't help but be curious. Apparently, his partner had left him too—she hoped in less humiliating circumstances than her ex, though she knew that would be scant comfort. She knew what it was like to plan a future, a happy family and a life together with someone. Since he already had a daughter, she supposed he'd been planning a life together too before the bombshell had dropped. Knowing he'd likely suffered the same heartbreak and bewilderment she had gave her a new insight into the man she would no doubt run into again in the future, now they were working in the same building.

'I can have a chat to him too, if that would help? I'm a hepatologist, so this is my area of expertise. I have some contacts who can provide him with counselling, or some rehab options.' Addiction wasn't something cured with a prescription or good will. It took a desire on the patient's behalf to want to change, but it also required some outside help at times. She'd referred many of her patients over the years to various services away from the hospital and, whilst it didn't work for everyone, lots of people had benefitted from different forms of therapy.

'Thanks, but I think I'll try and get through to him first. He's a stubborn so-and-so. I know how to handle him.' When he saw her tense at the merest hint she wasn't up to the battle, he added, 'I wouldn't want you to get offended if he goes off on one.'

That comment didn't do anything to appease her. It only served to remind her of their initial meeting. Then she saw the same twinkle in his eye and realised he was goading her. The growl of frustration which came out of her mouth was as unfamiliar to her as it was amusing to him, as she pushed past him back into the cubicle, ignoring the chuckling behind her.

'Mr Jackson, I think we're going to have to keep you in overnight. Do you have anyone we can contact for you?' She watched Liam walk back into the cubicle, waiting for him to challenge her authority. Although she didn't officially start until tomorrow, and technically this was his jurisdiction, she was very much invested in this patient and his future.

A brief frown marked Liam's forehead before it disappeared again. 'We're running a few blood tests while you're here to see if there's anything else going on inside that body of yours.'

'I thought it was a clean break. Surely all I need is a bit of plaster and some crutches?' Ray was already trying to sit up, probably planning his escape to the nearest pub.

'The leg fracture should be a straightforward matter. However, it's your drinking that's causing us concern.'

Ray rolled his eyes at Liam's assessment.

'I'm a liver specialist, Mr Jackson, and I would like to keep you under observation tonight until we get the results of these tests. We might need to do a few body scans too, just so we can get a clearer picture of what's going on inside. Dr O'Conner has told me that alcohol may have been a factor in your fall today and, combined with the colour of your complexion, it gives me reason to think you might have some liver or kidney problems going on.' The whole time Mae was giving her talk, Ray was glaring daggers at Liam for throwing him under the bus.

'So, it's a crime to have a pint now, is it? It's St Patrick's Day, in case you hadn't noticed. The whole country's enjoying a drink today. Well, apart from you two, obviously.' Arms folded across his chest, Ray looked as belligerent as they came, but Mae was used to dealing with people in denial. They usually only ended up under her care because they'd been ignoring the signs of the toll alcohol was taking on their body, completely in the grip of their addiction, until it was obvious to everyone else around them. By the time they reached her door, they were experiencing severe repercussions of their lifestyle choices.

Of course, not all her patients were in the thrall of addiction; many had illnesses or congenital problems they had no control over. That was why she found people like Ray so challenging and frustrating. They'd had choices. Okay, so life wasn't as simple as saying yes or no to a drink or doing drugs, otherwise the world wouldn't be populated with people lost to their vices—but there was still time to turn their lives around. Too often they had no interest in doing so, content to take the easier path they'd grown accustomed to rather than doing the hard work it took to make the change.

'If it was just one drink we wouldn't be worried, Ray, but we all know it's more than that.' Liam was deep into his 'serious doctor' mode now and Mae could only imagine how often he'd first used the friendly approach to try and get his neighbour to slow down the drinking.

'What else have I got to look forward to if I can't have a beer?' he complained.

Mae might never understand that all-consuming desire for the next fix of alcohol or pills, but she knew how it felt to face that dark abyss, believing nothing good was ever going to happen again. After the wedding that never was, she'd spent some time there, wallowing in the grief for her mother and the loss of her relationship; realising she was destined to be on her own for the rest of her life.

Perhaps it was the strength of character she'd inherited from her mother which had pulled her out of that despair, and for that she gave thanks and counted herself lucky to have had such a badass role model. Not everyone was able to claw their way out of that quagmire, and she was sure her mother had languished there herself once upon a time, as a single parent in a foreign country. After all, she'd left behind her life in Ireland to follow her American tourist love, only to be left with a baby in a foreign country when he'd grown tired of family life. Not unlike Mae's situation, though thankfully she didn't have a child to bring up alone.

But the Watters women had managed to pick themselves up, dust themselves off and build up stronger defences than ever, which hopefully would prevent another emotional collapse. Especially now she'd sworn off serious relationships, negating the risk of ever being blindsided, humiliated and rejected by someone who was supposed to love her.

'There is a life outside of the bottle, Ray. I don't mean to sound patronising, but I think if you have a few days of clarity you'll come to the same conclusion yourself.' Mae knew she was playing with fire, especially when they weren't one hundred percent sure how bad Ray's addiction was. Even Liam had seemed surprised that he'd been drinking so early in the day, so perhaps he wasn't aware of the full extent of the man's difficulties. She didn't want to cross the line, especially when she was only starting her new job, but she wanted to help.

'I can't stay. You know I have to get back for Brodie.' Ray deferred to Liam as threw off the bed covers, clearly not intending to stay put.

'His dog,' Liam clarified.

'He's not just some wee dog that can be left alone. Brodie's an Irish Wolfhound who'll probably be wrecking the house as we speak. He doesn't like being left on his own.' It was clear Ray was using his pet as an excuse to leave, but Mae knew if he left now they'd likely never get him back for another investigation.

'I'm sure someone can look in on him—or, failing that, there are places we could phone to take care of him until you're discharged.' She was desperately trying to come up with answers to pacify him, and failing.

Enraged by the suggestion, he was now pulling himself up into a sitting position on the bed, trying to manoeuvre his injured leg so he could stand up. 'There's no way I'm giving my dog up. He's all I have. He's the only reason I get up in the morning. He has a routine and won't do well without me.'

'Wait, Ray. I can look in on him when I go home. Give me your keys and I can feed him and take him for a walk.' Liam's suggestion at least made Ray pause for thought.

'What about when you're at work? You know he likes company. I can't stay. No way.' Now Ray was on his feet and not even Liam, standing blocking his path, appeared to be enough to prevent him from hobbling away.

'I'll help too. I'm sure me and Liam won't

always be working at the same time, and it's only going to be for tomorrow, right? I can take a book and sit with him for a while after my shift. These tests are important, Ray.'

Mae surprised herself with the offer, but she was desperate, and she could see by the concern etched on his face that Liam was too. Minding a dog for a few hours didn't seem like a high price to pay if it meant improving the quality of a patient's life. Not that she'd be volunteering to pet-sit for every lonely patient that crossed her path or else she'd end up be-friending every cat lady in the city.

Both men were looking at her as though she were mad.

'You would do that?' Ray asked quietly, and it broke her heart to think that giving a few hours of her time to help him out was such a big deal to him.

'Yes.'

'That's settled. Ray, get back onto the bed, and Mae and I will see to Brodie. Happy St Patrick's Day.' Liam grinned and she couldn't help but think he'd somehow got the better of her.

* * *

This had been a bad idea all around. At first Liam had found some satisfaction in the idea of the haughty American trying to wrangle his next-door neighbour's giant mutt. It didn't seem so funny now that she was encroaching into his personal space. With both of them heading the same direction, and having volunteered to look after Ray's beast of a dog, he hadn't had much choice but to travel back with her to pick up Shannon and head home.

'After you.' He held the pub door open for Mae, half-expecting a lecture about how she didn't need anyone holding doors open for her. Instead, she tipped her head to him and walked in as though it was her local, without a hint of trepidation.

'It's not what I expected,' she said, glancing around before taking a seat in one of the booths.

'No? Not enough diddly-dee music or leprechauns leaping about for you?' he teased.

On cue, the traditional Irish penny-whistle music his mother liked to put on for visitors suddenly filled the bar. Mae chuckled, her shoulders heaving with every laugh at his expense.

'It's for the tourists, you know,' he tried to explain, fighting to be heard above the piercing tunes and Mae's deep, warm laugh.

In other circumstances, he might have been embarrassed at being shown up like that. He'd had enough of being made to look foolish when his partner and his best friend had been carrying on an affair right under his nose. It had been difficult to face people in public after that, wondering who'd known, and if people had been laughing at him behind his back.

With Mae, it was different. This game of trying to get the better of one another was a private joke between them—one that he was in on, not the butt of—and so far, this one-upmanship was the basis of their newly formed relationship. For work purposes only, of course. He wasn't interested in anything else so soon after his recent heartbreak.

Apart from anything else, bristly Mae didn't seem the motherly type, and that was something he would definitely be looking for in a potential partner—a sign that he'd found a soul mate who wanted to settle down and emulate his parents' happy marriage, which he envied. He'd thought when Clodagh had fallen pregnant that that would be the beginning of his dream coming true. He'd not realised that, instead of finding someone who wanted to settle down, his partner was someone whose head would be turned by a flash surgeon who only cared about his own wants, with no guilty conscience about splitting up a family.

'Well, you can tell them I'm not a tourist. Not any more.' She fixed him with an intense stare, but beneath it he could see the hint of a smile. This was how they'd butted heads earlier, but thankfully she appeared to have forgiven him for being a clumsy big oaf. Still, it wouldn't hurt to butter her up, in case he needed her help in the future at the hospital, or during their spell of dog-sitting.

'What can I get you to eat and drink? I'm not sure we've got any of the green stout left but I'm sure we've still got some boiled bacon and cabbage.' He couldn't seem to help bait-ing her, although he knew to stay away from the matter of her own heritage. It was clearly a touchy subject, and no wonder, if she'd recently lost her mother. Liam's family were so supportive of him and Shannon, he'd feel as though he'd lost a limb if anything ever happened to either of his parents.

'I'm fine, thanks. If you just want to take me to Ray's house to meet the famous Brodie...' She clearly couldn't wait to get out of the place but he knew his mother would never forgive him if he didn't make an introduction. She'd be offended if he brought someone into the family business and she didn't have the opportunity to show off her hospitality skills.

'All in good time. There's no way my ma is going to let me go without a feed in me. Besides, I'll have to wait until Shannon has had her tea as well, before I can go. Now, what can I get you to drink?' He wouldn't dare to presume.

'White wine would be great, thank you,' she said, apparently resigned to the fact they were staying for dinner.

'Good choice.' Liam made his way over to

the bar, keen to put their order in before the crowds of hungry tourists descended in earnest after a day in the sunshine.

He also wanted to chat to his mother to explain the circumstances. As someone who was always pushing for him to meet someone else, it would be easy for her to get carried away with the idea Mae was someone more than a new work colleague, and he wanted to nip that notion in the bud.

'How's Shannon been?' he asked, helping himself to a chip out of the basket his father was just plating up with some tasty-looking steaks.

'She's upstairs with your mum having something to eat. I'm glad you're here; I need her down here to help me serve up the food.'

'Shannon?'

'Your mum, you eejit.' His father gave him a good-natured clout around the ear for winding him up. He was never too old to tease them, or for a slap when he deserved it.

'Can I get two plates of pie and champ?' His stomach was rumbling. Usually by now he'd have had sampled most things on the menu, but events had overtaken his appetite, and he hadn't eaten since breakfast.

'Two plates?'

'Yeah, I've got a new work colleague with me. We had to miss most of the parade to go to the hospital.'

'The girls said there'd been an accident. Everything all right?' His father stopped stirring and slicing long enough to show his concern.

'Ray had one too many before he decided to head up the parade dressed as St Patrick, wearing stilts.'

The busy chef resumed his duties, shaking his head. 'I won't serve him in here any more. He's only hurting himself.'

'I know. I've had a chat with him and we're keeping him in overnight. Meanwhile, I'm helping to look after Brodie.'

His good deed earned a hearty laugh. 'Good luck with that.'

Liam helped himself to another chip. 'I know. Shannon will enjoy it, though. I'm just going to pop upstairs to see her and mum. We're sitting over at table two by the door— the redhead in the white coat.'

As Liam opened the swing door to go upstairs, his father leaned his head round to gawp at his companion, and gave an appreciative whistle and nod.

'She's a colleague, Da,' he reiterated before disappearing upstairs to repeat it all over again.

Mae sat people-watching whilst waiting for Liam to return to the table. It wasn't quite the quiet, reflective day she'd expected to have, but perhaps that wasn't a bad thing, when she'd started to spiral into grief, thinking about her mum before Liam and his daughter had rudely crashed into her self-pity.

She envied the jovial atmosphere the customers exuded, standing at the bar, waiting impatiently for their drinks. Every now and then the general hubbub was interrupted with raucous laughter or cheering as those dressed head-to-toe in green, or sporting fake ginger beards, egged each other on in stupid drinking games. They were clearly here for 'the craic', as they said around these parts, whereas she'd come to the parade to reminisce about those fun days she'd had with her mother. At least battling with Liam and Ray had taken her mind off more depressing matters.

She watched a man dressed in chef whites walk over, older than the other members of staff behind the bar, carrying a glass of wine and a glass of something dark.

'Thank you.' She accepted the wine as he pushed it across the table but nearly choked on it when he sat down in the seat opposite.

'My boy tells me you work at the hospital.' Ah, so this was Mr O'Conner senior.

Although the realisation that this wasn't an ageing stranger hitting on her helped ease her anxiety a bit, it was clear he'd come to check her out on his son's behalf. She didn't want to be rude, or make a bad impression, but she certainly wasn't in the market for commitment with a man with a small child.

'Yes, I'm a liver specialist. I went with him to make sure Ray, his neighbour, was okay.'

'That's bad business, that,' he said, shaking his head. 'He hasn't been the same since his wife died. A bit like our Liam. Since Clodagh ran off with his best mate, he's focused all his attention on Shannon and work. I mean, he's always been a good dad, but he doesn't make any time for himself, you know. He's still young and, if the women swooning over him in here are anything to go by, he's still a catch, wouldn't you say so?'

It was easy to see where Liam got his charm from, as his father gave her his best crinkly-eyed smile and put her on the spot.

'I, er, yes, I suppose he is attractive.' There was no reason to deny it. She had eyes—the dark hair, blue eyes and hint of scruff around the jaw was certainly an arresting sight. It was when he opened his mouth she found herself spluttering to find words.

'That's nice to know. You're not too bad yourself.' Liam chose the optimum moment to embarrass her, in earshot of the compliment she'd been duped into giving. In that moment, she was too mortified to process the one he'd paid her in return.

He set a plate of food in front of her, and another on the other side of the table. 'Da, you're in my seat.'

His father got up, not a bit put out by the discourtesy of his offspring. 'Sorry, what's your name again?'

'Mae.'

'Nice to meet you, Mae. I'm Paddy.' He held out his hand and waited until she shook it.

'Hello, Paddy.'

'Are you married?'

'Okay, Dad, that's enough of the inquisition. We're just here to get a bite of dinner then go and see to the dog. Don't you have a dinner rush to see to? There's a queue of people waiting to be served over there.' Thankfully, Liam's distraction seemed to work as he drifted back over across the bar floor.

'Nice to meet you, Mae. Hope to see you again.'

She raised her glass to him but he'd already disappeared into the throng.

'My dad,' Liam explained a little too late as he dug heartily into his dinner.

'I figured. I didn't order any food, though.' She looked down at the mound of mashed potatoes and spring onions paired with a huge slice of juicy meat pie.

'I did. We haven't eaten all day, and my parents would never let you leave without a meal anyway. It's champ with steak and ale pie. Eat up.'

Mae poked at the chunks of beef in meaty gravy encased in flaky pastry and cautiously took her first forkful.

'It's delicious.' Though she didn't think she could finish the huge portion, there was no denying the rich, dark steak pieces and creamy mash were tasty.

'See. How long since you've had a home-cooked meal?' he asked once he'd swallowed down his mouthful.

'I cook,' she protested. 'But you know the hours are hectic. I suppose it's been a while since I made anything substantial.'

She had to admit she was more prone to batch cooking once in a wonder, then freezing the results. So, more often than not, dinner was zapped in the microwave after a long shift at the hospital.

'Now you know where to come. Especially if you're going to be in the neighbourhood seeing to Brodie.'

'Sure.' She had no intention of running the risk of seeing Liam or his family again. As nice as his father seemed to be, and his mother probably was, she didn't want to be involved in their happy family set-up. She'd been doing just fine on her own this past year.

They both tucked into their meals and Mae realised she was hungrier than she'd thought.

'Sorry about my dad, by the way. Mum will likely be the same. They're not used to me bringing anyone in here. Though I did tell them both we're merely work acquaintances.' He stopped eating long enough to press home the point, fixing her with those piercing eyes.

'It's fine. My mum used to be the same, always trying to marry me off to any eligible bachelor.' Perhaps that was why she'd jumped into an engagement so soon after her mother had passed, trying to fulfil her wishes that she'd find a man and settle down. Thank goodness she hadn't been alive to witness the debacle that had been her wedding day.

'I suppose he told you the whole sorry saga about me and Clodagh?' Although he asked the question casually, Mae wasn't sure if he'd be hurt to know his father had indeed been telling a complete stranger about his failed relationship. She certainly wouldn't have wanted hers to be common knowledge. That was part of the reason she'd moved here, so she could be anonymous again, and not the poor, jilted fiancée who'd been left standing at the altar.

In the end she decided to be honest. It wasn't as though Paddy had gone into great detail about his son's personal life. He had no reason to. 'He just mentioned that she'd gone off with your best friend. Sorry.'

She was surprised when he smiled.

'It's not your fault Dad's a blabbermouth, or my partner and best friend were lying cheats. Most people at the hospital know anyway, so I'm sure you would've found out at some point. It's been a year—well, eleven months, two weeks and a day, to be precise. You'd think I'd be over it by now. Although, since we met in here during a karaoke night, it's hard not to think about her every time I set foot in this place.' He was trying to brush it off but Mae could hear the bitterness behind his words.

She recognised it. Although her ex hadn't cheated on her, as far as she was concerned he'd still betrayed her. He could have saved her the humiliation she'd felt in a church full of people they knew if he'd only had the courage to call things off before then. He'd taken some leave since, and actively avoided her, though she'd spotted him once or twice at work. He'd never offered a face-to-face apology, or a full explanation, other than a brief note to say sorry and that he simply wasn't ready for marriage. The actions of a coward she was glad she hadn't married in the end.

Once she'd got over the heartache of their relationship ending so abruptly, their future together being over without her having a say, she'd been left with a seething rage inside her. To this day she would find it hard not to punch him in the face, should she ever set eyes on him again. She wondered how Liam had restrained himself from doing the same to his so-called friend, or if indeed he had.

'It must have been very difficult. Especially when you had a daughter to think about.' Mae considered confiding about her own relationship disaster, so he didn't feel so bad about sharing, but it wasn't something she was ready to talk about yet when it was still so raw.

'At least one of us did,' he muttered under his breath.

'Does she see her mother?' It was none of her business, yet Mae found herself drawn to this little family. Probably because this was the most conversation she'd had outside of work in months.

'Not as often as she should, but it's a little awkward, I guess. She's still with Colm.'

'Ouch.'

'Yeah. Mum and Dad do the handovers every second weekend, so we don't have to see each other, but I know Colm, and he isn't a family man. I can't see him wanting to give up his Saturday nights out to watch cartoons and eat pizza with my daughter.'

'Sounds like my idea of a good time,' Mae joked, when she could see how difficult the whole situation was for Liam to talk about.

She was rewarded with that dazzling smile. 'Mine too. I suppose we'll get into a routine at some point and we'll find our "new normal". It's just taking a while to get used to.'

'When's the last time she saw Shannon?'

Liam screwed up his face, deep in thought, so she knew it hadn't been recently. 'About two months ago, I think. She took her to the cinema. Had her back by lunchtime.'

'At least Shannon still has her mother in her life. I know it must be difficult for you, but it's the best thing for her. I may not have children of my own, but I know what it's like to only have one parent in your life. My dad disappeared out of mine when I was little, so I never knew him. I don't even know what he looks like. I think that's what made losing mum harder—knowing I still have a parent out there, but one who doesn't want to be in my life. Shannon will appreciate you putting your own feelings to one side to accommodate the relationship she still has with her mother when she's older.'

Over the years, she'd sometimes blamed her mum for her father's absence, thinking she could have done more to keep him in their lives, or tried harder to find him. Deep down, Mae had to accept her father simply had no interest in having a daughter, and that was no one's fault but his.

At least Liam was trying to find a solution to his change of circumstances. All she'd done about her problems was run away from them.

'I hope so. I need a reason for maintaining contact with Clodagh other than some ember of hope that we can still make things work and be that happy family I convinced myself we were.'

Her heart broke for him. That sudden thump of realisation that a relationship was over hurt badly, left a person dazed, confused and struggling to figure out what had happened. She couldn't imagine still having to see her ex twice a month and pretend as though he hadn't ripped her heart out and stomped on it. It was the reason she'd moved to the city in the first place. Liam was stronger and more courageous than she could ever hope to be. Or else he was simply just a good father.

The woman who'd identified herself as Shannon's grandmother when Mae had handed her over earlier appeared in the bar with the little girl. Both had Liam's amazing eyes and dark hair, though he'd obviously inherited his height from his father's side of the family.

'You must be Mae. I'm Moira, Liam's mum. I think you already met Shannon.'

'Yes. Hi again, Shannon. It's good to see you both in nicer circumstances.' The last time she'd seen them, she'd been desperate to get away to treat the injured Ray lying in the middle of the parade. It had been a hasty explanation about how she'd been entrusted with Moira's granddaughter before she'd handed her over and disappeared into the melee.

'I hope he hasn't been making a nuisance of himself and showing us up.'

'Not at all. Liam has been very accommodating.' At least, he had since the hospital.

'You got something to eat and drink, then?'

'I did, thank you. It was delicious.' Mae's compliment drew a flush of pleasure to the woman's cheeks.

'You're welcome to stay for a few drinks. I don't mind Shannon staying overnight if you two want to hit the town.' Moira's gaze flicked between Mae and Liam and his sigh was audible.

'I've told both you and dad, we're just colleagues. Mae's only here to help out with Ray's dog. Now, have you got all of your stuff ready to go, Shannon?' Liam was on his feet, ready to go.

'Everything's in the bag and she's had her dinner.'

'Thanks, Mum.' Liam kissed his mother on the cheek and took the rucksack from her.

'Are we really going to see Brodie?' Shannon asked, her eyes wide with excitement.

'Yes, we need to feed him for Ray. Mae's coming with us, if that's okay? She's going to be looking after him for a while too.'

Mae just knew, if his daughter had had any objection to her being there, Liam wouldn't have hesitated to rule her out of the equation, quite rightly putting Shannon's feelings above all else. She admired that about him, even if there were other aspects of his personality which managed to irritate at times.

'Yay!' Shannon clapped her hands but Mae imagined that was more to do with her excitement over seeing the dog than her accompanying them.

Liam lifted his car keys. 'We're just a few minutes away. My car's parked around the corner.'

'You're driving?' Mae knew the fondness for alcohol on today of all days, and was surprised he'd take the chance of driving his daughter, even if he'd only had a couple of beers.

A puzzled frown marked his forehead. 'Yes. Why wouldn't I?'

'You've been drinking,' she spat out of the side of her mouth, so no one else would hear.

The frown deepened. 'Soft drinks only. Do you really think I would put my daughter in a car with me if I was drunk?'

Liam was almost shaking with the effort it was taking not to explode with rage. She could see it in the tension of his body, the set of his jaw and the flash of anger in his eyes.

She'd messed up.

'Sorry, I just thought with you spending so much time in the pub…' She trailed off, knowing there was no way of justifying the fact she'd jumped to conclusions.

'My Liam's not a big drinker, and I certainly wouldn't let him drive Shannon around if he was.' It appeared she'd managed to upset his mother too with her quick, inaccurate judgement. The last thing she wanted to do was offend the family when they'd been so warm and welcoming to her.

'I know; I'm sorry.'

'It doesn't matter. Come on, Shannon.' Despite his assurance it wasn't a matter worth dwelling on, Liam walked out of the pub without another word, pulling his daughter along by the hand.

'It was lovely to meet you. Thank you for your hospitality.' She gave Moira a weak, apologetic smile before following the pair out of the door.

As Liam buckled Shannon into her car seat in the back of the car, Mae waited patiently on the pavement to attempt another apology. Liam closed the door and turned to her.

'Okay, so now I can see why the stereotype thing was annoying. You're not just a Yank claiming she's Irish because her great-granny once ate some colcannon, and I'm not a drunken Irish lout. Can we start over?'

She was so relieved his anger had been short-lived, and that he'd owned up to being irritating to her this morning. It showed a strength of character she didn't usually come across. She doubted Liam was the sort of man who would have stood her up at the altar and let her find out their relationship was over at the same time as the rest of the congregation. He was the type to be upfront and honest, someone who wore his heart on his sleeve. If she ever thought about dating again, those were the first and foremost qualities she would look for in a potential partner.

But she wasn't, so it didn't matter. And why was she thinking about Liam and dating in the same context? He was a new work colleague, he had a daughter and he clearly got his kicks from pushing her buttons. Everything she should avoid at all costs.

She couldn't work out how she'd ended up in his car, with his daughter in the back seat, on her way to dog-sit for his neighbour, but she did know it was asking for trouble.

CHAPTER THREE

LIAM HESITATED BEFORE turning the key in the lock and took a deep breath, not sure what might be behind the door, or what he and Mae had got themselves in to.

'I have to admit, I haven't been inside Ray's house since his wife died. I have no idea what we might be walking into.'

'How bad can it be, right?' Mae shrugged but she was hanging back on the front step next to Shannon, waiting for him to take the first step inside.

They found out as soon as he opened the door. The stale smell of dog, beer and cigarettes hit them all at the same time.

'Wow.' Liam took a step back.

'Goodness.' Mae held her hand over her nose.

'It stinks in there,' Shannon declared very undiplomatically as she screwed up her nose.

'Let me go in and open a few windows.' The gloomy hall suggested Ray hadn't even opened the curtains, never mind the windows. He meant for Mae and Shannon to wait outside, but they followed him in, so he didn't have time to clear a path through the empty bottles, cans and post all lying in their path.

'He can't come back to this.' Mae began picking up the litter. 'Is there a recycling bin?'

'There should be one out the back. I'll go and get it.' Liam walked through the debris field in the kitchen to retrieve the recycling bin from the yard. The yard hadn't been looked after any better than the inside of the house, three-foot-high weeds sprouting from the cracks in the paving.

'Where's Brodie?' Shannon asked when he returned.

'I don't know. Maybe he's in the lounge. I'll check.' He left them filling the bin with the empties and braced himself for whatever else was in store.

The door was barely open before he found

himself flat on his back with a hound licking his face enthusiastically.

'Brodie, I presume?' Mae was standing above him, not trying very hard to keep the smile off her face, whilst his daughter was laughing hysterically beside her.

'Uh-huh. Get off me, you stupid mutt.' It took some effort to prise the beast off him so he could stand, only to have Brodie jump up on him again, his huge paws landing on Liam's shoulders.

'He's not a mutt, he's gorgeous.' Mae ruffled Brodie's scruffy grey fur, earning her a new fan.

'I suppose we should feed him. I'll show you where everything is then you can go. Shannon and I will walk him.'

Mae's frown stopped him from planning the rest of the rota.

'I'm not going to go now and leave you to tidy this place on your own. We can hardly let Ray come back to this. It's certainly not going to do anything to improve his mood.'

'I can't ask you to clean up this mess.'

'You didn't. I volunteered.'

He was surprised someone as well turned out as Mae would even offer to dirty her hands in a stranger's house. If he'd known it was this bad, he would never have brought her here. In future, he was going to have to keep a closer eye on his neighbour, who obviously wasn't coping well on his own.

'Okay. Shannon, can you play with him while we're in the kitchen?' He didn't have to ask twice. She was already digging into the pile of dog toys in the corner and throwing them for Brodie, who was quick to switch his loyalty.

'Will she be all right with him?' Mae hovered in the doorway, apparently reluctant to leave the scene.

'He's a big softy, honestly. She plays with him all the time. I wouldn't leave her in there otherwise.' Liam was doing his best not to take offence, as it seemed his parenting was being questioned once more, and chose instead to believe Mae was simply concerned.

'I know. Sorry.'

As far as he could tell, she worried a lot about other people. Why else would she be here now, helping to clean a patient's house? Ray wasn't her friend or neighbour, just someone she knew was having some trouble at home. They'd all been complete strangers to her until this morning and there weren't many people who would have got involved outside of their work commitments. It showed she had a big heart, and was possibly as lonely as he was, if she had nothing better to do with her evening.

She hadn't mentioned having to get home to anyone, not even a pet—something most people would've used as an excuse to get out of cleaning, and he wouldn't have blamed her if she had. It was different for him: he knew Ray. He should have realised there was more going on other than him drinking one too many and too frequently. As a doctor, he should have seen the signs of depression, which had obviously set in after his partner had walked out, and the potential signs of liver disease. Perhaps he had been too wrapped up in his own problems and self-pity to notice. Now Mae had helped him to peel back the layers to see what was going on behind the scenes, he felt as though he had a duty to be a better friend and neighbour to Ray.

'So, Brodie's food is in this cupboard, his food bowl stays in the kitchen and his water bowl in the living room.' Liam set about filling the bowl before starting in on the kitchen clean-up.

Mae was brushing up the dog hairs littering the floor whilst he began the mammoth task of washing the dishes. It looked as though Ray had used every plate and glass in the cupboard without ever thinking to clean one. He shuddered at the thought of whatever germs lingered on the cluttered, dirty surfaces.

'You're quite the domestic god, aren't you?' Mae teased as he scrubbed the pots clean.

'I've had to be, since it's just me and Shannon at home. It wouldn't be fair to have her growing up in this sort of mess. Doing the dishes was always my department, anyway. Clodagh was afraid of breaking a nail. Although, I will admit to buying a dishwasher since she left; I'm not super-human.'

With only him doing the household chores and taking care of Shannon, he'd had to make better use of his time, as well as asking for help from his parents when he'd needed it. Despite trying to do everything on his own at first, it had soon become apparent that he couldn't juggle parenting and work all on his own.

'I have a dishwasher and I live on my own. Time's too precious in between shifts to waste it washing dirty plates,' replied Mae. That answered one question, at least, though Liam couldn't help but push for more. After all, she'd learned more about his family circumstances over the course of one day than most people who knew him. He only thought it fair he should know a little more about her too.

'So, what are you doing, wasting it here? It's your day off; you should be out celebrating somewhere.' He wasn't blind, or stupid. Mae was an attractive, successful, caring woman. There had to be men, and women, desperate to spend time with her. Liam was sure it wasn't a lack of interest that was keeping her in the singles market and wondered what had happened to make her think it was a better choice than being with someone. It was certainly to do with heartache: he knew the symptoms.

'I've not long moved to the city. I don't know many people yet, and to be honest I'm after a quiet life these days. The past months have been a little fraught, to say the least.' That sad look in her eyes, the sigh of resignation and her apparent need to hide away from the world suggested a recent break-up. He'd gone through the same stages after Clodagh and he wondered if she'd reached the rage part of the process yet.

'Oh? New start in the big smoke?' That was one thing they didn't have in common. Born in Dublin, Liam had lived there his entire life, and had never wanted to live anywhere else—except when Clodagh had left, when the moon wouldn't have been far enough away for him to be from she and Colm, his so-called best friend.

Mae, on the other hand, seemed a more adventurous soul, having travelled from America in the first place. He couldn't imagine moving to a different country and not know-ing anyone, not having that support system which had got him through some of the dark-est days of his existence. Whatever had hap-pened, it must have been serious enough for her to leave what was familiar to her to start all over again in another country.

'Yeah, but not in the exciting "Boston girl moves to Dublin" way you probably think it is. I didn't get sick of the country life, it got sick of me.' She gave a half-hearted attempt at a smile and Liam could almost feel the pain it caused her even to fake it. Kind of like when he'd promised Shannon everything was going to be all right, and desperately tried to hold things together at the same time.

'You want to talk about it?' It had taken him a couple of days before he'd admitted to himself, never mind anyone else, that Clo-dagh had walked out on him. But, when he had finally confided in his parents, it had been a relief to share the burden—to spill all the hurt and betrayal he'd felt, his fears for the future and worries about Shannon. They'd helped to quell the panic in him, promising to help where they could, and that was when the tide had begun to turn. He'd been able to see a future, albeit different from the one he'd planned with Clodagh. Eventually he'd managed to get some semblance of a life back together, even though the scars would always remain.

Although he couldn't promise to do as much for Mae as his parents had done for him, he hoped a listening ear might go some way to easing the pain. She deserved some help after everything she was doing for Ray.

'No. Yes.' This time he knew the smile was for him.

'I think it's only fair, when you've had all the gory details of my relationship laid bare in the space of a few hours. It puts me on something of a back foot when we're going to be working at the same hospital...'

'I would never say anything!' She had such a look of horror on her face at the mere suggestion she would use any personal information against him that he had to confess, it was simply another attempt to get a rise out of her. He couldn't seem to help himself.

'I'm joking. It's my defence mechanism when I think things are getting too serious. Probably part of the reason Clodagh had enough of me. She always said I needed to grow up. How ironic is that, when she left the father of her daughter to run off with the hospital playboy?' His thoughts began to drift back to the shadows of the past and he was grateful when Mae scooped some suds from the sink and flicked them at him. A distraction from his relationship woes was always welcome.

'I must remember that. It'll save me from losing my temper with you so often.' She nudged his elbow with hers so he could see she hadn't taken offence—this time.

'I am serious about offering a shoulder to lean on. Here, have this one; I'm not using it at the minute.' He slouched one shoulder down and she leaned her head on it for a split second before they both burst out laughing.

It felt good to do that again—to have a brief moment of happiness when he wasn't worrying, or over-thinking. And it was nice to have someone to do it with, even if Mae was only here because of Ray. If it hadn't been for the accident and her insistence on being involved, he doubted she would even have spoken to him again unless forced into it.

Mae's laughter soon turned back into another sigh. 'It's hard, isn't it, to just pick up and move on? How do they do it? Where do they get the audacity to ruin someone's life and walk away without a care in the world?' Now she really was beginning to get riled, and he was glad this time it wasn't because of something he'd done. That fiery red hair certainly matched her temper, that feisty nature revealing more about her Irish heritage than her DNA.

'I guess some people just don't have a conscience.' He could never have lived with the guilt of cheating on Clodagh, never mind walking away and leaving her to raise their daughter alone. From what he could tell in the short time he'd known Mae, she would never have acted that way either, when she couldn't even imagine letting Ray walk back into a dirty house.

She was quiet for a moment, as if debating

internally whether or not to share something. Gazing out of the window, not meeting his eye, she spoke so softly he nearly missed it. 'I was jilted at the altar. Literally.'

Liam didn't know what to say; it was such a shockingly cruel thing to have suffered. He supposed this was how she'd felt when she'd heard about Clodagh's betrayal. No words seemed adequate to convey just how sorry he was that this had happened to her.

'That's awful. I thought that only happened in films. You know, the ones where the heroine gets her revenge in the final act and her deadbeat ex gets his comeuppance?' He didn't know how else to make things right for someone who clearly deserved to be treated better, other than to try and make her smile.

Liam had hoped the image of her ex losing everything, or being humiliated in a similar fashion, would ease the pain a little, but it didn't.

'I wish. Unfortunately, I'm still in the "licking my wounds" phase.'

Sometimes, in his low moments, he fantasised about his ex-best friend being dumped for someone more exciting and carefree to see how he liked it. Not that it achieved anything other than to put Liam in a bad mood. He hadn't reached the stage where he wished any harm to the mother of his daughter, and he wasn't sure he ever would. He was probably still in love with the idea of the little family they'd been, rather than Clodagh. He also had to accept some of the blame for their relationship breaking down, he supposed. The fact he'd remained oblivious to her seeing his friend right under his nose said how little they'd communicated, or had even been involved in each other's lives.

In hindsight, they'd been ships that passed in the night at times, his shifts often clashing with Clodagh's work at the local hotel, though he'd never know if that was intentional or not. He'd been under the mistaken impression they were still working as a team and hadn't realised she was unhappy after eight years together. Perhaps he simply hadn't wanted to believe it, if it would have meant admitting his family wasn't as perfect as he'd imagined. Clodagh had had a point about him never growing up when he'd still believed in the fairy tale and the happy-ever-after, thinking it happened by magic. Not that it took work and communication to maintain a healthy, happy relationship. He was only realising that now, too late.

'It passes—eventually. I'm so sorry he put you through that. Assuming he wasn't a cruel man who intended to embarrass you, I can only assume he simply didn't have the balls to tell you he didn't want to get married. I'm sure it wasn't anything you'd done, or deserved. He must just have left it too late to fix things and you suffered as a result. I think I'm guilty of doing the same thing with Clodagh—ignoring the strains in our relationship until it finally snapped and there was no way of fixing things. By the time I had to face reality, she'd already moved on.'

'Were you married?'

He shook his head. 'I proposed several times, but she said she didn't need a bit of paper to verify our relationship; that having Shannon was proof enough, even though we hadn't planned her. I suppose not wanting to get hitched to me was a blessing in disguise, or a sign she never intended to stick around—I'll never be sure. But I wanted the wedding, and thought we'd even add to our family some day. I guess we were both on different wavelengths. I wanted to settle down and commit, Clodagh was looking for a way out. I just didn't want to see it.'

Mae was listening intently, and he realised giving her a shoulder to lean on had also made him take a closer look at what had happened to Clodagh and him. Yes, she'd broken his heart along with his trust, but there had been signs. On occasion she'd tried to arrange date nights for them to 'talk' on the rare evenings they'd both been at home, but more often than not he'd spent that time at his parents' place. Talking about his feelings hadn't been his strong point—at least up until they'd been ground into the dust. When Clodagh had given up asking him, he'd assumed she was okay with the close relationship he had with his family. That was probably when she'd given up on them, and had moved on to his so-called best friend.

Mae shrugged. 'Perhaps we're both just romantics at heart. Both oblivious to any problems because it would ruin the fantasy. I think the reason I got so upset when you called me out about moving here to find myself a husband was because it was true. I was lost without my mum and, when I met Diarmuid at a medical conference, he represented everything I was missing in my life. I followed him back to Ireland looking for something to fill that void. It was asking too much, apparently, putting pressure on him that he couldn't handle. I learned my lesson about relying on anyone but myself for my own happiness.'

There was a resignation in Mae's voice that he knew was a defence mechanism because he'd just built one himself, determined not to let another person close enough to inflict that level of damage to his heart ever again. He wasn't sure how long he could sustain it, when his tragic heart still held out hope for that happy family he'd always longed for.

'You deserve more, you know.' He stopped washing the dishes to turn and look at her properly, trying to instil his sincerity and that belief into her psyche, willing it to go beyond the insecurities her ex had left behind.

She gave him a wobbly smile. 'We both do.'

Perhaps it was the proximity to one another, or that recognition of one wounded soul finding another, but something seemed to happen between them—as if a switch had been flicked, awareness suddenly crackling between them. Liam knew she was beautiful but in that moment he saw her frailty, her vulnerability, and he found himself inexplicably drawn to her. Especially those sweet lips she'd just parted with the tip of her tongue, as if waiting for him to show her the tenderness she did deserve.

For a moment it seemed to him that the only sound in the room was of their breathing, rapid and ragged. Anticipation and expectation filled the air between them. He was going to kiss her, he wanted to kiss her… and her eyes and lips said she wanted him to kiss her.

Then he heard Brodie bark, Shannon laugh and he came back down to earth with a bump. He'd only met this woman this morning; he had a daughter to think about, and he couldn't go around kissing random women in front of her. She'd been through enough turmoil, for him to start confusing her like that. It wasn't as though he even wanted to start a new relationship with anyone, so kissing Mae was a really bad idea—as tempting as it was.

He stepped back without saying a word and saw Mae compose herself again, the moment over.

They continued with their chores in silence, the unburdening of their souls, and their almost kiss, clearly taking its toll. If he was honest, he was a little embarrassed to have revealed so much personal information to someone he'd only met, and he suspected Mae felt the same way, even if they'd both clearly needed to vent. It was also probably the reason they'd nearly kissed, finding a solace in one another that they hadn't had with anyone else since having their hearts broken.

It was a relief when Shannon and Brodie came charging through the door, breaking the awkward atmosphere that had settled in the kitchen.

'When can we go home, Dad? I'm tired.'

'Very soon. I've just got to feed Brodie.'

'Why don't I do that and let you get Shannon to bed? I can take Brodie for a walk before I go home.' Mae was giving him an excuse to leave, and Liam would take it. He needed some time to regroup, to think about what he had told Mae and, more importantly, why. It was clear they had a lot in common, despite initial impressions, but he didn't want to get into some kind of dysfunctional therapy-based relationship where, every time they saw one another, they'd lapse into introspection about their break-ups, bemoaning their exes…or thinking they'd found the solution with their lips. It wasn't going to help either of them move on.

'You can leave the key under the mat for me when we're done. I'll see to him in the morning.' Then, hopefully they'd only see each other in passing at the hospital.

For someone who'd sworn never to let anyone into his heart again, he'd opened the door wide enough for her to have a peek inside after just one day of getting to know one another. He couldn't afford any more slip-ups.

CHAPTER FOUR

Mae had an emotional hangover. She hadn't slept well and, quite frankly, felt ill thinking about how much she'd shared with Liam yesterday. And what she'd almost shared. It would be easy to put her effusive diatribe about her marital humiliation down to it having been an emotional day for her personally. She'd been upset about having the first St Patrick's Day without her mum, and in her home town.

However, deep down, she knew the reason she'd told Liam all the gory details was because he was another jilted unfortunate. The circumstances might have been different, but they'd both been left hurt, scarred by the betrayal of their trust. In her defence, he had spilled the gossip on his doomed relationship first, and she'd known he wouldn't judge her for having been rejected so publicly. Her greatest fear was that other people would side with her ex, believing he'd had a lucky escape, and that there must have been something wrong with her for him to have walked out on their wedding day.

If anything, Liam had made her see the fault had been on both sides. He'd accepted some of the guilt for not having seen the signs his relationship had been in trouble and, when she looked back, she could say the same. She'd been the one making all the wedding preparations; Diarmuid had never really got involved. Talk about their future had been a one-sided affair at times, and she'd put that down to cultural differences—Irish men weren't really known for being great at expressing their feelings. Well, she'd been partly right—he simply hadn't been able to tell her he wasn't ready for marriage.

Yesterday had been a revelation. Once they'd got over their first meeting, talking to Liam had felt like talking to a friend. It had been therapeutic, in a way. Being able to confide in him was akin to the valve in a pressure cooker being released. It was as though all the hurt, rage and confusion she'd been left with these past months finally had somewhere to go and it had all come pouring out—unfortunately for Liam. She'd clearly mistaken his empathy for something more and thought he was going to kiss her at one point, embarrassing them both. In the end, she could sense he'd been glad of the excuse to get away from her when she'd offered to walk the dog.

So she didn't understand why he was at Ray's bedside now, knowing she'd be here.

'I know visiting time's over but I sweet-talked the nurses into letting me see Ray. Please don't chuck me out.' He batted long, dark eyelashes at her, which were almost as mesmerising as the bright blue eyes they framed.

She held up her hands. 'I'm just here to give Ray an update.'

'You can say whatever it is that has put that frown on your face in front of Liam. He's the only visitor I've had.' Despite the circumstances, Ray didn't appear to be feeling too sorry for himself. Rather, he seemed resigned to the bad news she'd come to deliver. It was the part of Mae's job she detested, but all too familiar in her line of work. Liver problems weren't often fixed with a prescription and a bandage.

She pulled the curtain around the bed to afford him some privacy and took a seat at his bedside. 'As you know, Mr Jackson—'

'Ray,' he corrected.

'As you know, Ray, we had some concerns about your liver function so we ran some blood tests. Unfortunately, the results of those tests suggest there's something serious, called alcoholic hepatitis, going on. We would like to do an ultrasound to get a better idea of what we're dealing with before we proceed in case there are any complications with the condition, and to rule out things like gallstones. You're also suffering from malnutrition. Alcohol suppresses the appetite, so you're not getting a well-balanced diet. We want to keep you here a little longer for investigation and to make sure you're well enough to go home.'

Ray nodded his head sagely. 'Am I dying?'

'We're nowhere near that conclusion. For now, we just need to see what's happening inside, then we can put a treatment plan in place. At this moment in time, there is no cause for alarm. If you're able to stop drinking completely, the liver can regenerate itself and undo a lot of the damage. We will refer you to a dietitian and a counsellor to help with that.' Although there was clearly an issue, it wasn't going to help having Ray worrying about it. They needed to keep him calm in the meantime.

'What about Brodie? I can't lie about here knowing he's at home alone.'

'He's grand, Ray. Dr Watters and I have been checking in on him. I'm sure another couple of days won't make much difference.' Liam looked to Mae for confirmation that they could make it work, given they both knew how serious Ray's situation could become if left to continue untreated—perhaps even fatal. It was something neither of them would want on their conscience, even if it meant the two of them coming into proximity outside of work for a while longer.

When she realised she'd hesitated too long, she spat out a quick, 'Of course. We'll look after him. I'll go around once my shift is done. He's no trouble at all.'

A little white lie she felt was needed in this situation.

'You rest up, Ray, and don't worry.' Liam rose at the same time as Mae.

'Easier said than done,' Ray grumbled.

'We'll do our best to take care of you, and Brodie,' Mae promised as she left him to rest.

Liam waited for her in the corridor. 'I didn't know it was so serious, otherwise we could have at least provided him with some proper meals.'

It was clear he was feeling guilty, but Mae knew he'd been too busy going through his own personal problems to keep track of his neighbour's health too.

'Does he have any family? I don't see any listed in his file but perhaps you know of someone who could be with him? It might not be a bad idea to have someone close by.

He'll need support to give up drinking altogether.'

'None that I know of. He never had any children, and he's never mentioned family. That's probably why he fell apart after his wife died. She was all he had.'

Mae could see how he'd fallen into despair so easily. At least she'd had work to distract her after losing her mum and Diarmuid in the space of a year. If she'd been stuck in the house alone day after day, she might very well have succumbed to the melancholy in some form or another. Losing a loved one affected so many aspects of a person's life, even their personality; she considered grief an illness in itself.

'I guess it's up to us, then.' She didn't see any way to disentangle herself from the situation now. She and Liam were inextricably linked, at least for the duration of Ray's hospital admission. Perhaps even after, depending on whatever ongoing treatment he needed.

Ray might find he was too exhausted after all his appointments to give Brodie the exercise he needed. Liam had admitted he needed extra help to manage Shannon and work, so it would be asking too much to expect him to do everything on his own, especially when Mae had no other commitments. After yesterday's heart to heart, he was aware she had no life outside of work, so she couldn't very well cry off helping now without it seeming as though she was avoiding him. Which was what she would prefer, given all that she'd shared with him last night. It would have been nice to have some breathing room, a little time and space for him to forget the most humiliating details of her personal life, and nearly kissing him, before they'd been thrown together again.

'Sorry. I know I should have asked before volunteering us both for Brodie duty again, but if I hadn't he'd have tried to discharge himself.'

'Not a problem. It's not as though I have anything else to do with my time off than keep an Irish Wolfhound company.' It was absurd, really, that a dog had a better social life than a city doctor but she supposed that had been her decision.

Since moving here only a couple of weeks ago, she'd cocooned herself in her apartment to protect herself from any other men with the capacity to break her heart. Like all her recent decisions, it probably hadn't been the best idea. She hadn't taken that time to meet new acquaintances and now she had no one to call for a chat, or with whom to go for a coffee. Perhaps she'd have to rethink her hermit lifestyle and try to make a few friends in her new job. Otherwise, she was going to have a very small social circle to call on when she needed company, which only included a single father and a needy hound.

'Thanks. Listen, about last night…'

Mae's insides bunched together at the mere mention of their time together, the thought of everything they'd shared in that kitchen coming back to haunt her. 'Let's not talk about it ever again.'

Liam gave a hearty laugh. 'Yeah, it was a bit full-on. I just wanted to say that I'm not usually so…open. I don't want things to be awkward between us when we'll probably see each other here at the hospital from time to time, and now that we're Brodie's full-time carers for the foreseeable future. Rest assured, I won't bend your ear every time I see you about my tragic personal life. That's not me.'

He omitted all mention of the almost-kiss and she was grateful. Hopefully they could put it behind them and pretend it had never happened.

'No, you're more likely to tease me until I lose my temper.' She couldn't resist putting him in his place about their first interaction which seemed much longer than only yesterday—though she was relieved to find Liam was also obviously having regrets over sharing so much yesterday. They'd clearly both needed to talk and had simply found themselves in a moment of weakness. She didn't think either of them would make the same mistake again.

Liam grimaced. 'You're never going to let me live that one down, are you?'

'No.' Not when she enjoyed seeing him squirm.

'Ouch. I guess I deserve it. Anyway, I guess I'll see you tonight.'

'Tonight? I thought it was my turn with Brodie. Aren't you working?'

'Not tonight. My, er, mother has invited you over for dinner. I know, I know, I told her we're just friends, barely even colleagues. I also made the mistake of telling her you're new to the area, and don't know many people here yet, so having a meal with the family is mandatory. Sorry.'

Mae could see from his eyes and the furrowed brow he wasn't any happier than she was about the situation but they were both committed to the event now. If he hadn't issued the invitation, his parents would have been upset, and if she declined they'd be offended. It seemed they were destined to spend another evening in one another's company.

'Hmm. Well, I'll agree on the basis that any talk about exes is off the table. I've done enough soul searching to last a lifetime, so I'd like to just enjoy a nice meal with your family without even thinking about Diarmuid.'

'Done.' Liam held out his hand for her to shake. 'Although, I can't speak for my mother...'

Her washing-machine stomach churned at the prospect of her having been jilted on her wedding day becoming dinner conversation for Liam's whole family. If they were anything like him, they had absolutely no tact or boundaries. Not a good match for a sensitive, self-confessed hermit.

'Thanks for inviting me over, Mr and Mrs O'Conner.' Mae handed over a lovely bouquet of pastel-coloured flowers to his mother, instantly earning her mega brownie points from his already over-keen parents.

Liam had been fielding questions since last night about where she lived, who her parents were and, most importantly to them, if she was single, and if so why. Not that he told them any of the personal information Mae had entrusted him with. He certainly wouldn't have appreciated her sharing anything he'd told her in confidence with anyone else, even if his parents had no such qualms.

'It's lovely of you to come. Doesn't Mae look beautiful, Paddy?' Whilst his mother brought a blush to their guest's cheeks, his father was battling the embarrassment of having to pay someone a compliment.

'Aye. Grand,' he muttered, before shuffling away into the kitchen in the flat above the bar.

Dressed casually in jeans and an off-the-shoulder white fluffy sweater, red wavy hair tumbling loose and wearing a pair of cowboy boots, Mae was beautiful. She also couldn't have looked more American if she'd tried.

Liam could understand why his parents were not so subtly pushing to get them together. On paper she was everything a man could want—beautiful, smart, successful; the list went on and on. It was just a shame neither of them was interested in a relationship after having been so badly burned by their last ones. Not that he was probably even her type, when she found him so irritating. Given what he'd heard about her ex, he imagined Mae's type was all talk no action, cowed by a successful, confident woman and clearly afraid of commitment—about as far removed from Liam's personality as possible.

None of which would dissuade his parents from believing that they should at least try—for his sake and Shannon's. Their belief that all he needed to move on from Clodagh's betrayal was another woman was jarring to say the least. As childhood sweethearts who'd been together for decades, they would never understand what it was like to have their heart ripped out the way he'd had. He was playing along tonight to keep them happy, but had made another attempt to convince them they were merely acquaintances before Mae's arrival.

It hadn't been a fun task, asking her over after last night, and he'd been afraid things would be awkward. Apart from their deep and meaningful conversation, he didn't want her to think he was pushing for more, either romantically or in terms of reaping added personal information. Thankfully Ray had given him an excuse to be in her department, at least, giving them more reason to spend time together. Liam was glad he and Mae had managed to get over any embarrassment and had made an agreement to veto any further talk about exes to make this evening bearable.

'You sit there beside Liam, Mae. Shannon, you sit beside me and Paddy can go at the end of the table.' His mother issued orders for the seating plan at the table in the small living room, leaving Mae and him exchanging a knowing look that said they'd go along with this to keep the peace.

'You really didn't need to go to all this trouble for me!' Mae exclaimed as his father loaded the table with dishes of chips, mash and veg, along with a selection of roast meats. A typical Sunday dinner, especially made midweek for their visitor.

'Liam said you've just moved to the city. This is our way of welcoming you,' his mother insisted as she took Mae's plate and filled it for her.

'But you fed me last night!' Mae laughed.

'Now you're a regular.'

Liam didn't even bother to hide the smirk on his face. His mother had an answer for everything when it came to getting her own way. Now Mae would see how they'd both ended up here tonight again.

She didn't argue any more, simply digging in to the mountain of food which was handed to her. She was learning fast. 'Well, thank you, Mrs O'Conner. You've certainly made me feel welcome.'

'Moira, please.'

'You need some veg, Shannon.' When he spied his daughter's plate consisted mostly of chips, Liam piled on some broccoli, much to Shannon's disgust.

'Don't you just love these?' Mae speared a floret on her fork and studied it intently. 'It's like eating mini trees.' She popped the whole thing in her mouth and chomped down.

Liam observed his daughter watching the whole thing, then she very slowly lifted a piece of broccoli to her lips and bit down. A couple of mouthfuls later, and the whole thing was gone. It was the first time in weeks she hadn't had a temper tantrum at the table when he'd tried to get her to eat anything remotely healthy.

He blamed himself for his daughter's predilection for junk food. When Clodagh had first left, he couldn't face cooking or eating, and it had been easier to order a takeaway for Shannon. Then he'd been trying to over-compensate for all the turmoil she'd gone through in the separation, letting her make her own meal choices for a sense of control and comfort. He'd wanted her to be happy, and he hadn't wanted to be the bad guy, forcing her to eat something she didn't like. However, as a doctor, he knew all too well that that would lead to consequences later on and meal times had become something of a battleground lately. Something not aided by his mother, who liked to spoil her only grandchild too.

Apparently, all he'd needed was an attractive stranger to make her think there was fun to be had in eating broccoli and she would be converted. He wouldn't complain, but he did wonder if he now needed to have Mae in attendance for all meal times. A good female role model wasn't to be underestimated and, though his mother spent a lot of time with Shannon, he wondered if he would have to rethink his current bachelor status if he was going to avoid further clashes with his daughter. She had yet to hit puberty, when there'd be those turbulent teenage years to come…

Mae gave him a wink across the table and he offered a smile in return, until he noticed his mother watching their interaction. Not wishing to give her any more false hope, he instead focused on clearing his plate.

'How's Ray? Liam said you'll be looking after that dog of his for another few days.'

Liam was relieved his mother's line of questioning wasn't focused on Mae's relationship status, at least.

Mae finished swallowing her food before she answered. 'Yes. We're going to be keeping him in to run a few more tests.'

He knew Mae, as Ray's doctor, wouldn't be comfortable sharing details of her patient's condition without his consent, so he did it for her. 'Ray's in a bad way, Ma. The drinking has caught up with him and he has liver damage. We'll know better once he's had an ultrasound to see how bad he is, and what treatment he'll need.'

He could see the news had shocked his parents, his mother crossing herself and promising to pray for him. His father remained silent but he knew he was simply processing the news. Sometimes it was difficult for his dad to reconcile how he and his mum made their living with the serious drinking culture that seemed to dominate the area. Although Liam knew they didn't serve those who had an obvious problem, some people, like Ray, hid it better, and his family shouldn't feel responsible for grown adults making the wrong decisions.

'Is he going to die, Daddy? What will happen to Brodie?' Shannon, who had been sitting quietly absorbing the conversation around her, now voiced her worries.

'We're going to give Ray the best treatment we can, that's why he has to stay in the hospital for a while longer. So we can make him better.' Mae chose her words carefully, trying to reassure Shannon things would be okay.

Neither of them could promise that Ray wouldn't die if he didn't stop drinking and, as much as Liam wanted to stop Shannon from worrying, it wasn't fair to give her false hope. It could make things more difficult in the long wrong if something did go wrong, and losing his daughter's trust would kill him.

'Mae's his doctor, so you know she'll take good care of him, and we'll look after Brodie for as long as we're needed. We won't leave either of them alone, okay?'

'Thanks, Daddy.' Shannon leaned across to give him a hug, so he knew just how much that meant to her.

He found himself welling up, not only at his daughter's compassion for their neighbour, but also at her display of affection towards him. Sometimes he really just needed a hug—another reminder that being on his own for the rest of his life wasn't something he wanted. One day he'd have to take that chance and risk his heart in the hope the gamble paid off. That he'd get that happy family he'd always dreamed about.

'Don't you worry your head, sweetheart. Mae and your dad will look after Ray, and Brodie,' his mother promised.

Shannon finished her meal, then asked to

play games on his phone, and he was pleased that their combined efforts to reassure her everything would be okay appeared to have had the desired effect. He supposed it was better that she'd asked rather than keeping her concerns to herself, but he realised he'd have to be more careful about what he said around her. She'd seen and heard more than she should at her age. Liam was ashamed to admit he hadn't reacted well when he'd discovered Clodagh's cheating, and there had been rows before she'd left. He was trying to make up for it, to be a better father to Shannon, and that meant protecting her from other people's problems where he could. She didn't need to worry about things that were beyond her control.

He could also do with taking a leaf out of his own book. Clodagh had made her decision, and what he'd done, or hadn't done, to contribute to that decision no longer mattered. There was nothing to be gained from continually castigating himself about the past. It was more important to think about the future and the life he and Shannon could still have. Just because things hadn't worked out between her mother and him, it didn't translate they could never have a happy family again with someone else.

What it did mean was that he had to be open to another relationship, had to be brave enough to open his heart again and make sure it was someone who wouldn't hurt his daughter or him again. It was a lot to ask, and a lot of that responsibility to make another relationship work would weigh heavily on his shoulders when he knew he'd been part of the problem in the failure of his relationship with Clodagh.

His talk last night with Mae had at least opened his eyes to the things he could've done differently, so hopefully he would learn for the future. If he'd only been able to talk to Clodagh the way he had with Mae—with honesty and by digging deep into those emotions he'd been afraid to voice out loud for so long—they might have been able to salvage their relationship. Now he could only hope he'd use what he'd learned about himself to improve a relationship he was yet to have.

The next step was to put himself out there again, show willing when it came to dating again—though he was worried that he might end up unravelling about his ex, the way he had with Mae, and put off any potential partners. He was lucky she'd even agreed to come here tonight, but he supposed that was only because they'd both made it clear that it was out of a sense of duty rather than a wish to be with each other. He was safe with Mae.

At least with her he didn't have to pretend he was holding it all together; he wasn't under pressure to impress or perform. Mae had seen him at his most raw, wallowing in self-pity and recriminations. Far from scaring her off, she'd been able to empathise with his situation. And she'd still agreed to come tonight. She must be as lonely as he was.

Despite her initial reservations about accepting Moira's and Paddy's invitation to dinner, Mae had enjoyed it. It was nice to be part of a warm, loving family, even for a little while, and they had made her feel as though she belonged there. It didn't seem to matter that she was an American stranger to them, with no romantic links or otherwise to their family. As an acquaintance of Liam, she'd been accepted regardless, and had been regaled with stories, jokes and an evening of excellent company. She was almost sad to leave, knowing she was going back to a house where she left the TV on constantly simply so there was some noise other than the sound of her own thoughts.

It was this need to replace the comfort of the little family she'd had with her mum that had most likely led her into her relationship with Diarmuid. A rebound of sorts, trying to replace one love in her life with another. It probably would never have worked long term, because Diarmuid could never have adequately filled the void her mother's death had left inside her. He hadn't been right for her, and eventually she would have seen it too. It just happened that Diarmuid had realised it first, even if he had gone the wrong way about breaking up with her.

Diarmuid had represented an escape from her grief, planning their marriage and future

together at a time when she'd been afraid
she'd never have one, fearful that she'd be on
her own for ever. Now she had to accept once
more that that was the more likely scenario
than that she'd ever trust enough to share her
life, and her heart, with anyone again.

After her father and Diarmuid walking
out on her, she didn't trust another man not
to do the same. No one could guarantee she
wouldn't end up alone and heartbroken again.
She'd seen it with her mother time and time
again: her dating, falling in love then being
left when the man had grown tired of the relationship, until she'd been left alone to deal
with her illness. Mae had been there for her,
of course, juggling her medical career with
her mother's needs, but she'd seen how upset
her mum had been because she'd been let
down again. Her latest beau had bailed out
on her once he'd known she would need a lot
of care.

If she did ever date again, it would be a casual thing, in which she wouldn't hand over
her heart and trust someone not to stomp it

into the ground when they tired of her. She needed to protect herself.

Still, that didn't mean she didn't miss the cosy atmosphere of a family dinner. She'd only known the O'Conners for a couple of days but they were becoming a familiar part of her new life in Dublin. It wouldn't be easy just to walk away and pretend they'd never crossed paths. She would always be drawn here any time she was in this part of the city. Whilst there was no problem in dropping in every now and then to say hi, she had to make sure she didn't confuse her relationship with Liam with her longing to belong...again.

However, Shannon was yawning, and she couldn't very well stay on after Liam went home just to feel part of something again.

'I think I need to go home and lie down after that. I'm full! But thank you for a lovely dinner.' Mae said her goodbyes, sure her waist had expanded a good two inches since she'd arrived.

'Any time, love.' Moira saw her to the door and kissed her on the cheek.

'Nice to see you again,' Paddy added.

'Shannon and I will see you down to the door. Night, Mum and Dad.' Liam hugged his parents and waited until they'd both kissed Shannon goodnight before he opened the door.

The moment they stepped out of the bubble, the noise of the outside world came rushing up the stairs to meet them: screaming, shouting, glasses smashing; it sounded as though war had broken out down below.

'I'll go and see what's happened,' Liam said, trying to usher Mae and Shannon back inside.

Moira took her granddaughter by the shoulders but Mae wasn't going to be so easily restrained. Both she and Paddy followed Liam downstairs.

'What's going on?' he asked the bar staff, who were standing staring at the open door.

'I think a fight has broken out from the pub across the way. Do you want me to close the doors before it spills over into here?' The hipster-looking barman, with a ginger ponytail and beard, clearly wasn't looking to get involved.

'No. There might be people hurt out there.'

'It's not our problem, son.' Paddy tried to dissuade him from getting involved but Liam was already holding open the door, ready to go out into the fray.

'I'm a doctor, Da. Of course it's my problem,' he said, before stepping out.

Mae followed him out, eager not only to help if she was needed, but also to make sure Liam didn't get into any trouble himself. It was clear that this was an ongoing issue between father and son: Paddy ran a self-contained family business he wasn't willing to put at risk for any reason; Liam, on the other hand, couldn't help himself from offering help, as she had seen yesterday at the parade—and probably even when it wasn't wanted or appreciated.

She admired his dedication to his profession, but also his bravery in wading in. If she'd been on her own when a drunken brawl had broken out, she couldn't be certain she'd be heading in the direction they were now. It was only knowing she had Liam as back-up that gave her enough strength to follow him out there.

'Somebody help. He's bleeding!' A clearly distressed and inebriated young woman was standing over a man sitting on the ground, blood pouring from his head turning his once white T-shirt a startling scarlet.

'Yeah? He deserved it. There's more where that came from.' A great, big oaf of a man, his belly drooping from underneath his too-tight football shirt, was staggering about in the middle of the street, waving a broken bottle.

'The Garda are on their way,' someone shouted from the crowd, which had backed away from the man with the makeshift weapon.

'Phone an ambulance too,' Liam commanded, advancing on the feuding pair.

'Liam, be careful.' Mae had no idea what he was planning, but her heart was in her mouth at the thought he was about to get in the middle of this nasty fight. He waved a hand behind him, and she wasn't sure if it was to tell her to be quiet or to stay back. It didn't matter because she didn't intend to do either.

'I just need to check your friend's head

wound. I'm a doctor.' Like a zoo keeper trying to wrangle a wild animal, Liam slowly edged forward on his toes, a hand out in front to demonstrate he meant no harm.

'This is none of your business.' The angry man waved the bottle in Liam's direction but the threat did nothing to deter him.

'I'm a doctor. It kind of is.'

'He'll live. That's what he gets for spilling my beer.'

'I'm sure he didn't mean it.' Liam nodded over to the injured victim, presumably trying to get him to make an apology in order to calm the situation.

No such luck.

'It's hard not to bump into him when he's the size of a flaming house.'

'Say that again!' The man lunged forward at the insult, and Liam jumped in between the pair.

Mae didn't want to watch; she couldn't even breathe, thinking that he was going to get himself into real trouble. But she wouldn't leave in case he needed her.

'Just give me the bottle, mate, so no one

else gets hurt.' Liam tried again to reason with him.

'I'm not your "mate". I'm nobody's "mate".' The big slug of a man jabbed the bottle at Liam.

Mae let out a scream, but Liam had jumped back at the last minute, so all the man managed to stab was air.

'Hey, you, you big bully, he's only trying to help.' Mae couldn't help herself. It wasn't in her nature to simply stand back and watch as someone got hurt, any more than it was in Liam's. Plus, he wasn't just someone. He was a colleague, and someone she'd begrudgingly become used to having around these past couple of days.

'Mae, what are you doing? Get back.' Liam was staring at her, madder than she'd ever seen him, brow knitted into a serious scowl and jaw clenched so tight, it looked as though he might actually break something.

'He can't just threaten people and get away with it. This man has a daughter, you know. He's a single parent, yet he's waded in here, trying to help. What does he get in return, someone trying to stab him with a broken bottle and take him away from her? What kind of country is this? What kind of man are you?'

Her rant at least distracted the attacker. He was probably wondering if he should make a charge at her to shut her up, but he did take his eyes off Liam and drop his guard for a moment.

It gave Liam the opportunity to make a grab for the bottle, catching him unawares. Although, once the thug realised what Super Doc was trying to do, he fought back, causing a tug of war between the two over the bottle. Seeing the situation was still precarious, and with no one else appearing to want to intervene, Mae launched herself at him. She jumped onto the man's back, digging her boots into his sides, covering his eyes with her hands, and generally trying to disorientate him. The burly guy did his best to shrug her off, but she clung on as though she was riding a bucking bronco, slapping him, kneeing him in the back and desperately trying to get him to drop the weapon. In the end, he had no choice, deciding it was more important to deal with her now.

That was when she realised she could be in trouble. Liam pulled the bottle out of his hand and threw it away, but not before he got a punch to the nose. The sight of the blood streaming down his face was enough to distract Mae and she let up on her assault for a moment, worried that he'd been seriously hurt. Her bronco took the opportunity to fling her off his back as though he was swatting a fly, sending her flying onto the cobbled street below. She landed with a hard thud, her backside taking the brunt of the fall.

Their burly attacker took one look at the chaotic, bloodied scene he'd created and took off, lumbering down the street, pushing people out of the way, but at least he was gone. The immediate threat had passed and, judging by the sound of the police sirens coming closer, it wouldn't be long before the Garda would pick him up.

'I don't know whether to hug you or shout at you for being so stupid.' Liam came over and held out a hand to help her up from the ground, the other pinching the bridge of his nose in an attempt to stem the bleeding.

Whether it was the shock of what had just happened setting in, the genuine concern she saw on his face for her or the sheer relief that he was okay, she didn't know, but she burst into tears all the same.

Liam helped her to her feet and pulled her into a hug.

'I'm going to get blood all over your lovely sweater,' he whispered into her ear, as the crowd gave them a round of applause for their efforts, before filtering back into the various pubs they'd exited to watch the show.

'I don't care. I need a hug.' She buried her head in the crook of his shoulder, luxuriating in the warm, manly feel of him around her. The security of his embrace was everything she needed after the drama and upset.

When the hug lasted a probably inappropriate amount of time for two people who professed to be work colleagues only, Liam let go.

'Er…if you're okay, we should probably go and check on the patient.'

'Yeah. Just a bruised…ego,' she said, patting her backside to make him laugh.

'It's fine, there's no need to fuss,' the man with the very obvious head wound insisted as they approached him.

'Let me clean it up and take a look for myself. We did just take on that maniac with a broken bottle for you,' Liam reminded him.

'Didn't ask you to, did I?'

'Don't be so ungrateful, Mikey. You could have brain damage or anything.' A woman who must have been his girlfriend gave him a slap on the arm, showing the most sense out of the two of them.

'This is all we've got inside, Liam. What the hell happened to you?' Paddy arrived carrying a first aid kit, apparently having missed his son's heroics. It was probably just as well or else he'd likely have joined in.

'It kicked off a bit. You should have seen Annie Oakley here, taking on the big guy wielding the broken bottle.' Liam took the first aid kit and began cleaning the head wound, ignoring his own injuries.

Paddy looked at her with a mixture of surprise and bewilderment. 'You tackled a man brandishing a weapon?' He turned to Liam. 'And you let her?'

'She wouldn't listen.'

'The guy was distracted at the time.' Mae tried to downplay her part in the melee, and the seriousness of it, neglecting to mention he'd been trying to stab Liam when she'd jumped aboard.

'Anyway, it looks as though the Garda have caught up with him.' Liam pointed down the street where the police were chasing down their assailant, tackling him to the ground and forcing handcuffs on him.

Mae was relieved they wouldn't have to worry about him coming back. She'd had enough excitement for one night.

'Let's get you sorted, then.' She moved over to where Liam was tending the patient.

'That's going to need stitches.'

'I'm not going to hospital. Sod that.'

'If you don't, that's going to keep opening up. We can only patch it up for now.' Liam dabbed around the wound with an antibacterial wipe, drawing a sharp intake of breath from his reluctant patient.

'It's a deep wound. Dr O'Conner is right, it needs stitches. An open wound could get easily infected and lead to more problems. Best to get it treated now.' Mae retrieved a sterile dressing from the first aid box and taped it over the large gash in his skull.

All they received in response for their efforts was a grunt, although his girlfriend did offer to buy them both a beer. By the time the paramedics arrived on scene, Mae was glad they were relieved of their responsibility.

'What about you, sir? You look as though you've been in the wars too. You might need a check over too.' One of the ambulance crew tried to persuade Liam to have some treatment, which she could have told him was a waste of breath.

'It's just a bloody nose. We're both doctors, so I'm sure we can sort it ourselves, can't we, Mae?' He looked at her to confirm he didn't warrant an ambulance ride and a wait in Accident and Emergency, despite the blow he'd taken.

Though she was tempted to throw him under the bus, both to tick him off and make sure he was all right, she knew he didn't want the hassle.

'Sure,' she said, with more enthusiasm than was believable, earning her a glare from Liam.

'Well, you don't want to go back in there. You'll scare Shannon.' Paddy used typical Irish humour to disguise any concerns he would have had over his son's involvement in the brawl.

'I know. Best not tell my ma, either,' Liam made him promise. 'I've got the keys for Ray's house and we have to sort the dog out anyway. I'll get myself cleaned up then come back for Shannon.'

'I'll pass on your details to the guards if you're sure you're both okay?' Paddy looked at Mae for reassurance before he was content to go back into the pub without them.

'We're grand,' she said, attempting her best Irish accent.

Paddy gave her a thumbs-up, leaving the scene at the same time as the paramedics with their uncooperative passenger. Now that the two of them were alone in the middle of the street, it seemed as if the whole thing had been a figment of their imagination. Except for the blood covering Liam's face and shirt and the bruises she could feel forming on her butt cheeks.

'So… Ray's house?' Mae packed up the rest of the first aid kit to take with them, hoping they wouldn't need to use anything other than some antibacterial wipes to clean Liam's face. The blood appeared to have stopped streaming at least since she'd plugged his nose with some cotton.

'Ray's house,' Liam confirmed, pulling the key from his pocket and waving it so close to her face she had to slap his hand away.

'You can be so annoying, you know.'

'Yeah, but you love it. Why else do you keep coming back for more?' Liam grinned.

Why indeed? Though she was grateful no longer to be so concerned about his wellbeing she felt physically sick, Mae knew there was a reason she was drawn to Liam. She did like him, regardless that he could push her buttons. He was that elusive combination of being fun and a friend—both of which had been missing in her life for some time. Liam and his family were refilling the well of good times and company that had been empty for too long, bar fight notwithstanding. It did mean they were going to be spending more time together alone, when the feelings she'd been having during the tussle tonight had been definitely more than a passing concern.

As long as he kept up this annoying man-child version of himself, she'd survive. Hopefully.

CHAPTER FIVE

'HELLO, BOY.' LIAM scratched Brodie behind
the ears as he came to meet them at the door.
'I think we'll bring him in next door for a
change of scenery while I get changed. I don't
want to drip blood all over Ray's house. Can
you grab Brodie's lead and food bowls?'

Mae located the dog's belongings, leaving
Liam to wrangle on the lead and pour some
food from the giant bag into the bowl, which
she carried next door. Liam led them all to
his house. As he turned the key in the lock,
Mae experienced a little flutter in her belly
as she was allowed over the threshold into
Liam's inner sanctum. There was a certain
intimacy in entering someone's home for the
first time—a trust that she had yet to place
in anyone sufficiently to let them breach the

sanctuary of her new place. Despite Liam having shared so much with her yesterday, she got the impression he valued his privacy. This was a privilege, even if she'd only been invited in because of the events tonight.

She followed him down the hall, where he flicked on the light, illuminating the homely kitchen. It was tidy except for the childish drawings and pots of paint littering the farmhouse-style table: the mark of a man who took pride in his home, yet wasn't afraid to let his daughter have fun expressing herself.

He took the lead off Brodie, which resulted in the dog doing a mad dash around the small kitchen, knocking over one of the dining chairs, before returning to jump up and lick Liam's face.

'Who's such a good dog?' Mae muscled in on the action, fighting for the wolfhound's attention. He was another one she was getting used to having in her life.

Brodie left Liam's attentions to enjoy Mae's cuddles. Ray hadn't mentioned any house rules so, after Liam and Shannon had gone home last night, she'd spent her first dog-sitting shift cuddled up on the sofa with Brodie, watching TV. He wasn't a fan of wildlife programmes, it turned out, restlessly looking for the animals who'd had the audacity to come into his house. However, he'd settled down when she'd put on her soap operas. Clearly he found it as comforting as she did that the people in the kitchen sink dramas had more problems than her.

Neither she nor Brodie would have expected to see each other again so soon.

'You're so fickle,' Liam chastised Brodie, who was standing on his hind legs, feet on her shoulders, nuzzling his head into her neck, not caring a jot what Liam thought about his swapping allegiance so quickly and easily.

'Ah, he loves me.'

'Huh,' Liam grunted. 'He loves anyone who'll feed him and pay him attention.'

'Me too.' Mae grinned.

'Then you must be head over heels for me.' Liam tossed the comment over his shoulder as he made his way past the love-in going on between Mae and Brodie.

It brought Mae up short. Whilst she wasn't

head over her heels for Liam, she knew she liked him. She just didn't want him to know that.

'For your family, maybe. Your dad can cook, your mum is *very* attentive and your daughter is super-cute. I'm afraid you're none of those things. Just…irritating.' She wanted to get the message across that she was *not* falling for him, then she set down Brodie's dinner so he'd love her a little bit more.

'Irritating, huh?'

'Also frustrating, and reckless when it comes to getting involved in fights that have nothing to do with you.' She added that one on behalf of his parents and daughter, who would've given him grief over his actions if they'd known what he was up to at the time.

'Ah, but never boring.' Without warning, he stripped off his shirt and ran it under the cold-water tap in a vain attempt to rinse the blood out of it.

She didn't know where to look. Well, she knew where she wanted to look. Her eyes were drawn to his broad back and the smooth muscles of his arms and, if she tipped her head forward a little bit, she could see the pert pectoral muscles.

'Do you want me to give you the full show?' He'd caught her red-handed. Her embarrassment was only topped by the provocative dance he proceeded to do, hands behind his head, thrusting his hips towards her.

Despite the heat infusing her face, she was enjoying the full, uninterrupted view of his lean torso. Then Brodie nudged her arm with his wet nose to remind her what she was supposed to be doing here, and it wasn't ogling a new work colleague.

'Get over yourself. I simply hadn't expected you to be getting naked. Some warning would have been nice or, you know, you could have stripped off in another room.' She huffed.

'I would still be half-naked, so...'

'Maybe I should just strip off my top half and expect you not to be surprised.' It was so unfair men got to whip off their shirts at the drop of a hat and everyone was supposed to be cool with it. What if she hadn't wanted to know what body was beneath the tight shirts?

It wouldn't have kept her up all night wondering. Now she knew exactly what he looked like naked from the waist up, sleep definitely wasn't going to come easily. For someone who apparently ate very hearty, carb-laden meals, he had no business looking that good.

'Feel free. I'm not about to stop you.' He leaned back against the sink, arms folded, with that smug look on his face that almost made her want to call his bluff, to make him blush and bluster and think about nothing else but her being naked too. Except she couldn't promise that would happen. Whether he'd be turned off by her curves, wrinkling his nose in disgust, or they got into a game of one-upmanship that led to them both ending up stripping off completely, she couldn't take the risk.

'Pig.' It was the only comeback she could come up with in the moment. Not particularly witty or relevant, but hopefully it would end any expectation that she might whip off her sweater just to prove a point.

'Spoilsport.'

Grr. She just knew he was grinning behind her back.

* * *

Liam always used humour to deflect when he was uncomfortable and this was no exception. It had given him a thrill to catch her watching him like that, with undisguised interest in his body, and boosted his ego. That was something he needed after having been unceremoniously dumped, apparently found lacking in personality and physicality. Okay, so Mae had called him irritating, but he knew she enjoyed their banter as much as he did, otherwise she wouldn't have accepted the dinner invitation tonight.

Of course he hadn't anticipated them being caught up in a bar fight, and having to bring her home to patch him up—another step further into his private life and a big deal for him, when the only other woman who'd been in this house, except his mum, was Clodagh.

It was the threat, or promise, of her stripping off which had nearly been his undoing. His imagination had run away with him in that moment, thinking about where that could lead, until his head had been full of kissing, of hands caressing each other's bodies then ripping the rest of one another's clothes off… That was when he deployed the humour missile, knowing that teasing her would defuse any heat before it even had a chance to catch light.

He gave them both some time to cool down and washed up the couple of dishes he'd left in the sink before he fetched the first-aid kit, along with a clean shirt, and started to clean himself up. The first splash of cold water over his face stung his nostrils and filled the sink with swirls of raspberry-coloured streams of water. The intake of air through his gritted teeth drew Mae's attention back to him from Brodie's dinner.

'Let me tend to that. You can't even see what you're doing,' Mae tsked, clearly still irked by him, but her nurturing instinct was too strong to ignore his plight. He'd take it. It wouldn't do to tick her off so much she wouldn't help him with the dog any more. Plus, she made his evenings much more interesting.

Liam hadn't realised how staid his life had become of late until Mae had appeared, shaken things up, and given him a reason to leave his house other than to feed the next-door neighbour's dog or go to his parents' pub, which was only a few minutes' drive away.

He and Shannon had been hurting so hard, trying to find a new normal, get into a different routine from the one they'd been used to, that they'd locked themselves away from the world. Perhaps it was a defence mechanism—keeping out all the bad stuff, staying where they felt safe. It had taken an uptight, smart-mouthed American to show him the error of his ways. He still had a life to live, and so did Shannon, and he couldn't take away her freedom, even if he was trying to protect her in the process.

Taking her to the parade yesterday had been the first time they'd done anything fun and spontaneous since her mother had left. Although Ray's antics had ended their day out prematurely, there had been snatches of the old them, just Daddy and daughter enjoying their time together, instead of being bogged down in worry about their future without Clodagh. He knew Shannon missed her mother, but she mentioned her less now as she got used to it being the two of them.

Mae had helped to extend their socialising, even if it had just been going to his parents and next door. At least that meant they still felt comfortable, being in familiar surroundings, regardless that Mae was brand new to them. He was surprised how easily his mum, dad and Shannon had taken to her. It made it so much easier to be around her, knowing they felt comfortable around her too. Even if he was feeling distinctly uncomfortable now.

He silently thanked them for providing him with another opportunity to see and talk to her again outside of the workplace. She was becoming the brightest parts of his days, which had been pretty damn miserable until recently.

They sat down at the kitchen table, which they'd cleared of all Shannon's art work. Mae took some cotton and was now dabbing away the rest of the blood around his nose. It was the tender look in her eyes, her gentle touch, that he was struggling with most.

He had his parents' love, of course, but that physical and emotional connection as she tended to him was something he'd been missing, probably long before his relationship had collapsed.

The intimacy between Clodagh and him had virtually disappeared. They'd barely been in the same room even to accidentally touch one another, never mind do anything else. He'd put it down to over work and stress on both parts. Long shifts and looking after a child was all-consuming, even harder when there was only one parent in the household. He'd spent so much time these last months being a doctor, father and jilted partner, he'd forgotten what it was like simply to be a man. To have feelings that weren't negative, or wrapped up in someone else's, was new, exhilarating.

What was more, Mae was no longer looking at him as though he was merely an irritant, or a patient, but a man. She was studying him the same way he was watching her—with interest. He offered a smile and received one in return, albeit slightly hesitant.

'Thank you, Mae. For Ray, for yesterday and for this.' For making him feel like a normal man, attractive and wanted, with desires of his own.

She held his gaze for a while, and with every second the air between them grew thicker with anticipation and tension. That same urge to kiss her as he'd had last night came rushing forward and it was all he could do not to act on it. Then she turned away on the pretence that she had to pack away the first-aid things right there and then and saved him from making a fool of himself.

'You should probably put on a shirt. You don't want to add pneumonia to your list of ailments. I doubt you can afford to get sick when you have so much on your plate.' She flitted around the kitchen like a nervy butterfly, putting the used cotton ball in the rubbish and cleaning the sink.

This skittish version of her was new to him. She'd been so self-assured, both in combat with him and in a medical setting. It was clear she felt unsettled and he was sure he was the cause. They'd both been left hurting after their last relationships had spectacularly imploded, but he didn't think they should suffer for their partners' decisions for ever. They hadn't deserved the way they'd been treated in the past, and they didn't deserve to be punished now, afraid to open themselves up to anyone else in the fear they'd be hurt all over again.

A little flirtation, acknowledging an attraction, shouldn't be something to fear. It wasn't going to help them open up emotionally in the future if they saw it as something destructive. Not communicating had been his downfall in the past and he didn't want that to continue for ever. Not when he still had hopes that some day he'd be in a happy, healthy relationship, raising the family he'd always wanted.

'I thought you liked this look.' He'd neglected to put on the clean shirt under the pretence that he didn't want to get blood on it until he was all cleaned up. Now he knew it was because he liked to see that look in her eyes, that appreciation of his body, and the ego boost it gave him. He moved over to where she stood, knowing he was invading her personal space, waiting for her to push him away or draw him closer.

'Stop it. Please.'

To Liam's horror, there were tears in Mae's eyes as she quietly pleaded with him.

'I'm sorry. I didn't mean to upset you.' He always took things too far and now he'd crossed the line, mistaking her kindness for something more. Immediately stepping away, he tugged the shirt on over his head and covered himself up. As much as he wanted to comfort her, hold her and apologise profusely, he knew she probably just wanted to leave.

'You didn't. I mean…it's not you.' She angrily wiped away the tears before they dared to fall. 'I just can't handle anyone else playing with my emotions.'

'I wasn't… I didn't mean to…' He threaded his fingers through his hair and tugged, deserving every second of the self-inflicted pain and more. Guilty of only thinking about himself as usual, he'd neglected to realise she hadn't been having as much fun as he had during the exchange.

'I know you were only teasing but I'm still

a bit raw after Diarmuid. Having these…feelings isn't something I'd planned. I know I'm just the silly American but please don't make fun of me.' She was shredding the wrapper from the antiseptic wipe she'd used to clean him up, obviously fretting about what had nearly happened. But he'd been right about her feeling the attraction between them too. Her tears and the flight response was the manifestation of her fear at admitting it.

'I wasn't making fun of you. I promise.' Suddenly, the anger over their situation welled up inside him until he wanted to smash things, though it wouldn't have done anything only upset her more. It seemed so unfair. Clodagh and Diarmuid weren't likely to beat themselves up over their failures. Especially when Clodagh had moved on to the next relationship before she'd had the courtesy to tell him theirs was over.

He had to make do with pacing the floor like a captive animal as he raged about the unfairness of it all. 'Why should we feel guilty or ashamed that we might actually fancy one another? We're not kids, nor are we the ones in the wrong.'

Now he knew that Mae wanted the same thing as he did, but was too afraid of making a fool of herself, he knew it was down to him to make the move. He crossed the distance between them in one step. Mae tilted up her chin to meet him as though she'd been waiting for him to come and claim her, and he did.

He captured her face in his hands, her mouth with his, and kissed her as though they were free from all the worry that seemed to dictate their every move, every thought. For those few seconds, free from consequences and future regret, he kissed her with every ounce of passion he felt for her, channelling every one of those hopes and dreams that his future wouldn't be marred by the failure of one relationship into one kiss.

Mae latched her lips onto his, tentatively dipping her tongue into his mouth to meet him, letting her hands slide under his shirt and around his waist, mirroring every one of his movements, until their bodies were entwined like jungle vines, stronger together than in isolation.

A need for more of this freedom from the usual intrusive thoughts in his head, more of Mae and this rush of passion she'd awakened inside him, spurred Liam's libido. This wasn't the time for over-analysing and worrying about the future; he wanted to stay in the moment. And the moment was telling him to be with Mae.

'Should we be doing this?' she asked breathlessly as he kissed his way along the curve of her neck, brushing her hair away so he could continue his pursuit across her shoulder.

She gasped when he dipped his head lower and pulled her jumper down to expose the swell of her breasts in her lacy white bra, but he knew she didn't want him to stop. Not when she peeled off his jacket and just this moment unbuckled his belt. That jolt of awareness slammed into him as her fingers traced the buttons of his fly and he had to take a moment to remember to breathe, to try and clear his head a little, before he embarrassed himself.

'Probably not.' His laugh was a little shaky, much like his legs and his breathing.

This had been unexpected, exciting, and he was going back for more.

With extra urgency their mouths clashed together and their hands tugged at one another's clothes, their breathing ragged, their want evident. Mae couldn't even think straight, and she didn't want to if it meant putting an end to this. She was enjoying it too much.

It was nice to feel wanted, to know she hadn't got carried away again imagining something that wasn't there. Okay, so this was never going to be her romantic fantasy come true. They'd spent half their time winding each other up, plus he was a single dad, both of which were not keys to a successful relationship. No, kissing Liam was simply a chemical reaction and nothing else. He was right: she shouldn't beat herself up because she found someone attractive; she hadn't taken a vow of chastity, or broken any laws. They were two adults enjoying each other's company.

It helped that he was an amazing kisser. She didn't know from one second to the next whether to expect him to be soft and tender, or hard and demanding, but she was enjoying both aspects of his attentions to her lips. It made her think of what he was capable of in other areas, and she found herself keen to find out first-hand, caution be damned. Neither of them wanted anything serious; both were likely on the rebound and in need of a serious ego boost, not to mention a physical release. She was sure it had been some time for both of them since they'd last had anything resembling a sex life.

The loud ring of Liam's phone had him break off the kiss as though he'd been scorched, spinning round to discreetly adjust his clothes as he answered the call, as though they'd been busted by someone walking in unannounced. Mae busied herself wringing the last of the water out of his T-shirt on the draining board, hoping she didn't look as dishevelled with lust as she felt. She was dizzy from the sudden cold turkey she was now undergoing after the withdrawal of Liam's lips from hers. It was surprising how quickly she'd got used to kissing him. It had been intoxicating.

'Yes, Dad, I'm fine. I'm, er, just cleaning myself up. Yes, you can bring her over. No, I'm not going to scare her. Okay, I'll see you soon.'

Mae scrubbed at the blood on Liam's shirt rather than try and make eye contact.

'Dad's on his way over with Shannon,' he said.

'I should probably leave before they get here.' Before she did anything else likely to get her into trouble.

'Are you really still going to pretend that this isn't happening?' He was so close she could feel his warm breath on her skin. Enough contact, apparently, for her body to go into meltdown.

He opened his mouth and she assumed it was because he was about to make another wise crack. She hadn't expected him to kiss her again. Her eyes fluttered shut, her heart picked up an extra beat and her lips parted to accept him, as though her body was already pre-programmed to welcome him at the drop of a hat—or a T-shirt. This time the kiss was fleeting, barely there, and possibly the most frustrating moment of her life. Give or take coming to terms with her ex's behaviour, and inability to have spoken to her at any point in time before she'd made it down the aisle.

He took a step back and smiled. 'See? You want this. You want me.'

Still worked up by the kiss, and waiting for the next instalment, her body was inclined to agree.

'You're so full of yourself.' She dipped into her bag of self-protecting aides and pulled out a handful of sarcasm to chuck back at him.

'I'm only stating the truth.' He reached out and brushed a lock of hair away from her face.

Mae's eyes fluttered shut and she revelled in the brief contact. 'But what would it achieve?'

So they had chemistry, but falling into bed after knowing one another only a couple of days would be asking for trouble. Especially when they had to work at the same hospital.

'Er…how about fun? Remember that?'

'Remind me. It's been a while.'

Now that she thought about it, it was something that hadn't been in abundance even before the ultimate rejection. The weeks and months leading up to the wedding had been spent agonising over every detail, worrying that everything would go to plan. There hadn't been much room to do anything fun in between work and organising the big day.

Perhaps that had been a large part of the problem between Diarmuid and her. Even if he had complained they weren't spending enough quality time together, she probably wouldn't have done anything about it, because her attention had been completely consumed with the wedding, on having the best day of her life and proving the romantic fantasy had come true. She'd neglected the reality of their situation too long and their relationship had flatlined as a result.

A good time hadn't been high on her list of priorities since then. That spot had gone to simply surviving.

'No commitment other than to make each other feel good.' He dotted tiny, ghost-like kisses down her neck, sending goose bumps popping up all over her skin.

'That does feel...sound nice.' He was scrambling her brain with every touch of his lips on her body.

'Mmm-hmm. Doesn't it?'

'But Shannon... Your dad...' As nice as this was, the pair were going to be here soon, and there was no way there would be time to fit in everything she wanted to do with Liam in that small window. If anything, it would leave her frustrated to start something they couldn't finish properly.

'I know. Tonight's out of the question. So, I have a proposition.' He stopped kissing her and retreated back into his own personal space, leaving her dazed and confused.

She needed the breathing room because she was so disorientated and under his spell right now, she would agree to anything.

'What?' Even to her ears she sounded breathless, as though she'd just run a marathon. Her heart was racing too, the exhilaration of the moment doing more to fuel the adrenaline in her body than any form of exercise. Well, almost any… Her thoughts drifted to whatever indecent proposal he had in mind and whether or not her heart could take it.

'Neither of us are in the market for a serious, long-term relationship. Let's face it, we'd probably drive each other up the wall. But, it's also clear there's an attraction here. One we would be acting on right now if my dad hadn't interrupted.' The devilish glint in his eyes only upped the level of Mae's frustration, unaided by the fact he'd yet to get to the point.

'Yes, and he's going to be here soon with your daughter.' *So get on with it!*

'I know we haven't known each other that long, that we're going to be working at the same hospital and have Ray as a mutual connection. Sleeping together could make things complicated. If we let it.'

'What are you suggesting?' She had been trying not to think beyond tonight, or let herself feel anything that wasn't in the moment. Now Liam was ruining the mood by talking about the future consequences.

Liam cleared his throat. 'A fling.'

'Excuse me?' For a moment Mae thought she'd misheard him.

'I don't see why we should deny ourselves some fun. We haven't done anything wrong and we deserve some happiness. But I also know we're both still hurting from our last relationships. I thought perhaps, if you agree, we could keep things casual. You know? See each other in private.'

'You want to be my booty call?' The idea had its appeal.

'We would be each other's booty call. No strings, or expectations, other than having a good time.'

'That's a big promise.'

Liam ducked his head with a grin, almost bashfully. It was nice to see that perhaps he wasn't as confident as he often portrayed. She liked seeing that softer side of him. It represented him opening up, letting that brash exterior slip so she could see a more vulnerable Liam. The one who didn't want to risk getting hurt again either.

'I just know we would have a really good time together.' He pulled her close, capturing the gasp of surprise on her lips with his. The kissing alone was sufficient to prove his point.

Except she wasn't usually that kind of girl. At least, not one who got involved with fathers of young children. He was showing her a way round that, so the level of commitment that would normally have required wasn't an issue. But she was already so involved with his family, it seemed impossible to separate, or juggle, those relationships. After Diarmuid, she'd made a promise to herself not to get involved with someone she could lose her heart to so easily. She didn't want to lose herself in that commitment to a relationship and, seeing how close he was to his daughter, Liam seemed the worst person to rebound with. Even if he was suggesting something a lot more intriguing than potential heartbreak. Although the thought of exploring all kinds of possibilities with Liam was tempting, she just wasn't sure it would be worth taking the risk.

'I don't know, Liam. It's one thing getting carried away in the heat of the moment, but this is a crazy idea you're asking me to make a logical decision about.' Now she'd been given time to think, all the red flags were waving in her face. She certainly didn't want to agree to something now, when she was wound so tightly with arousal for him, only to regret it when her brain wasn't so fried by lust.

There was a rap on the back door as Paddy appeared with Shannon.

'Sleep on it. We can talk about it tomorrow,' Liam whispered, before going to greet his daughter and reassure her everything was okay.

There were so many things wrong with that last comment, but they wouldn't have the privacy to go over her fears now the rest of Liam's family was here.

Namely that there was no way she'd sleep tonight with erotic images of Liam in various stages of undress roaming unbidden in her head, and the prospect of more if she chose. Plus, she didn't think she could face talking about it again tomorrow without being affected by what had happened here tonight. Common sense told her she should put a stop to any romantic notions now and rule this as an error of judgement, a moment of madness which definitely should not be extended indefinitely. However, deep down she knew she wasn't strong enough to say no to this once-in-a-lifetime opportunity.

CHAPTER SIX

MAE HAD BEEN ignoring his texts. Liam had briefly considered calling and leaving a voice message when she invariably didn't answer his call, then decided it would seem too needy—the opposite of the arrangement he'd proposed. He still couldn't quite believe that he'd suggested a fling, or that she'd even agreed to consider it. Clearly his libido had been doing the talking last night, afraid that he wouldn't get to finish what they'd started.

He wasn't sure how this would work on a practical level when they would have to co-ordinate work and his responsibility as a father. It wasn't as if he could parade Mae through the house in the mornings and not expect Shannon to notice. The logistics would be difficult, though he couldn't bring himself to regret anything when she'd said she'd contemplate the idea of a fling.

It had been a last grasp to maintain the momentum which had sprung between them in the kitchen—not the most romantic place on earth, but it hadn't stopped them from engaging in one of the most passionate encounters he'd ever experienced. It was all he'd been able to think about, along with the possibility of having something more with Mae.

He knew a relationship was off the cards. Neither of them was emotionally ready to jump into anything serious, but it was clear they still had needs. A fling seemed the easy solution to fulfil their want for one another, and the ego boost might even help them when they were ready to move onto another relationship. They could avoid all the complications of family getting involved in their personal business by keeping it quiet, and it would give him something more than dinner with his parents to look forward to.

The only problem with his sexual master plan was the growing suspicion that, in the cold light of day, Mae had changed her mind and decided she didn't even want a casual fling with him. If she was agreeable to the idea in theory, he was willing to find a solution to ensure they could spend time together. Whether that meant meeting at her place, or booking rooms by the hour when Shannon was in school, he wanted to make this work.

From the second he'd made the suggestion, he hadn't been able to think about anything else other than being with Mae. Although a rejection from her wouldn't be the same as Clodagh leaving him for his best mate, it would still hurt. It would also make things awkward when he had to consult her on a patient and he still hadn't had her answer. That wasn't the sign of someone who couldn't wait to embark on a racy, passionate fling.

'Is there any update on Dr Watters?' he asked the head nurse, who'd been the one to put in the call requesting Mae's expertise. Whilst Liam knew Mae wouldn't have blown him off when it came to a patient— she was too professional—his behaviour last night had been anything but, and he could only hope that wasn't the reason she'd been avoiding him.

'Why don't you ask her yourself?' Liam's A&E colleague nodded to the space behind him.

He took a split second to compose himself, to brace for the look of contempt that was likely there on her face, before he turned around. But she was too hard to read when she was in doctor mode. Hair tied back, not a strand out of place, wearing a smart skirt and blouse, she looked immaculate. A far cry from the flushed, dishevelled version of Mae from last night. He knew which one he preferred: the Mae who couldn't keep her hands off him, not the one standing here with an indifferent expression on her face.

'I'm here. What do you need me for?'

It wasn't a loaded question for anyone but him. He needed her for company, for kissing, for feeding his ego, and hopefully for more. Although, judging by this cool reception and her refusal to reply to his messages, he'd be lucky if she even let on she knew him.

'We have a patient coming in who's taken

an overdose of Paracetamol. I can handle it, but I thought it would be good to get your input to try and limit the liver damage.' He'd known Mae was in today. They'd cross-checked their schedules to work out the times for looking after Brodie and he remembered there was a brief cross-over period this afternoon when they would both be in attendance.

Though he didn't take any joy in the fact someone had felt so desperate they'd thought to end their life, it gave him a chance to see Mae. She was also the best person to have on hand in this instance. An overdose of Paracetamol could result in potentially fatal liver damage. They only had a very small window of time to help and they were all lucky to be able to utilise Mae's expertise.

He'd seen more than his fair share of drug overdoses due to prescription and illegal drugs in the emergency department, accidental or otherwise. Some had been too late for medical intervention no matter how hard the staff had tried to provide assistance. Those were the cases he took home with him, the names and faces he couldn't forget because he felt as though he'd failed them. Even if Mae didn't want to speak to him personally, he'd willingly set aside his pride to have her here if it meant saving someone's life.

That invisible hum of tension before an emergency admission hung in the air. Everyone waited to launch into action the moment the doors swung open, powerless until they did. When the familiar fluorescent jackets of the ambulance crew blazed brightly as they crashed into the department with their patient on a stretcher, the hospital staff circled, ready to take over. They quickly transferred the patient onto a hospital bed, accepting the responsibility for the young woman's life, and relieving the ambulance crew so they could move on to their next job.

'Twenty-six-year-old female: Anne Marie Hagen. History of depression. Found unconscious by her best friend after breaking up with her boyfriend. Apparently surrounded by empty Paracetamol packets. She's breathing but hasn't retained consciousness.'

As always, the initial transfer was noisy

and busy, getting all the details of the case, and doing a preliminary assessment.

'Do we know how long ago this happened?' Mae asked.

'Her friend saw her about two hours ago, so it can't be that long.'

'Okay, thanks. We're lucky we got to her so quickly. Anything past eight hours would have limited what we can do.' She went on to order the usual bloods and urine sample, with the most important results being the liver function.

'Are you happy to go ahead with administering activated charcoal?' Liam asked, monitoring Anne Marie's blood pressure and pulse to make sure she didn't suddenly deteriorate.

He hadn't asked Mae to attend just so he could take over. He trusted her judgement, an expert in this field, but he wanted to be useful.

'Yes, and can we get an IV of acetylcysteine set up, please? Given that we're still within that time frame, we should be able to prevent serious hepatotoxicity.'

It didn't matter that this girl had tried to

take her own life; they would work together to save her as best they could. She was a patient, someone who'd clearly been so distressed she hadn't seen any point in continuing. It was always difficult when such young people were involved: they should have had their whole lives ahead of them. Now, thanks to Mae and everyone else involved, she still did. Of course, Anne Marie would have to be referred to the mental health team, but that was for her own benefit. Hopefully they would help her move past whatever issues had led her to make this choice, so she wouldn't ever try this again.

Although they couldn't know for certain if a break-up had been the catalyst for this, Liam understood how totally devastated she must have been to have attempted to end her life. When he'd discovered Clodagh and Colm in bed, he'd thought his life was over too. He hadn't seen a way past it and it was only having to look after Shannon which had forced him to get up out of the doldrums every morning and go through the motions of a functioning adult. Inside, though, he might as well have died. Suddenly his whole life had been taken away from him. He didn't know who he was any more, or what to do without Clodagh there. There had been a grieving period; it was only natural after the loss of a relationship.

He was still in the angry phase, and he just knew Anne Marie would get there too once she'd had a little time to think things through. The overdose had probably been an impulse reaction, a way to shut down the pain. Perhaps, as in some cases, it had been a cry for help—a signal to those around her that she wasn't doing okay and needed more support. With Mae's assistance, and a follow-up treatment plan, he hoped Anne Marie would eventually be able to put the whole thing behind her and start over, the way he had.

Yes, he still had some kinks to work out when it came to his love life—namely that he needed to find the courage to invest in another relationship. He imagined that would happen faster if Mae agreed to this crazy arrangement where they could have all the benefits of a relationship without having to commit their hearts to it, playing it safe.

'Okay, that should keep her stabilised for now. I'll want to see the results of the liver function test to see what we're dealing with, and she'll need a referral to psych.' Mae was winding down her part in procedures and Liam knew she wasn't going to stick around longer than necessary, to avoid talking to him. He didn't want to let that happen without a chance at least to clear the air in case he never got to speak to her again.

Mae was ready to leave, to get away from the sad circumstances of the patient that had hit too close to home, and the man she hadn't been able to get out of her head since he'd kissed her.

Suddenly, alarms were going off and medical staff swarming back around the bed again.

'She's gone into cardiac arrest!' one of the nurses shouted, forcing Mae immediately to turn back.

'We need a defibrillator over here!' Liam

yelled, waiting as the patient's clothes were cut open to give access to her chest.

He started chest compressions, keeping the blood pumping around her body until they could apply electric shocks. After a while he stopped to check for a response, but it was soon clear they would have to use the defibrillator to try and restart the woman's heart. Once pads had been attached, Mae took up the paddles. 'Stand clear.'

Making sure no one was touching the patient or her bed, liable to get a shock themselves, Mae delivered the first shock. She waited to check the heart rhythm but, with no improvement, responsibility transferred back to Liam.

Again, hands locked, arms straight, he began more chest compressions. He flicked a glance at Mae, which she didn't want to acknowledge. It was concern that they weren't going to bring this patient back after all. Mae had to retain a certain professional detachment at work, but in circumstances like these it was impossible not to be affected.

This was a young woman who'd had her

whole world in front of her. Yet, she had come to think, for whatever reason, that her life was no longer worth living. Mae knew that feeling. Running from the church, after realising Diarmuid wasn't going to turn up, it had crossed her mind to throw herself in front of the nearest bus. Then she wouldn't have had to deal with the loss, the humiliation and the heartbreak her fiancé's actions had caused. If she hadn't had her mother's strength, the outcome of those first few days after their breakup could've been very different.

These painful personal dramas, which seemed so all encompassing at the time, did eventually become easier to live with. She only hoped Anne Marie got the opportunity to realise that, to see she could still lead a very full life.

Liam stopped CPR to check the patient's heart rhythm, then it was Mae's turn again.

'Stand clear.' She delivered another shock with the paddles, watching Anne Marie's body jerk as she did so.

It seemed like such a violent act, but she'd seen time and time again how it often gave people a second chance at life, and she only hoped this woman would be one of them. Life was short. Certainly too short to give up on it at such a young age.

She thought of Diarmuid and herself. In a way, she'd been guilty of giving up her life for him, even though she was still functioning on an outward level. Moving away had been a start, as had getting herself a new job, but in terms of her personal life she might as well have died. It was only natural she'd wanted to protect herself, but she'd basically let Diarmuid win. She'd decided that he was the only man who could ever mean anything to her. She really didn't want to live with that for ever. He'd gone on to have another life. They both deserved the same—to move on from the heartbreak and start living again.

Suddenly, the expectant air around the cubicle was filled with the steady beep of Anne Marie's heart, and Mae had to fight back tears. They'd done it. Now this woman had been given another chance at life, it would be down to her to move on from the past and look to her future. Mae knew she had to do the same.

'Let's get her stabilised.' The medical team swung into action, getting her settled again, though she would probably be transferred to the intensive care unit once she was stabilised so they could keep a close eye on her. Hopefully, once they got all the toxins out of her body, she would be well on her way to recovery.

'Thanks for your assistance, Mae... Dr Watters,' Liam said to her once their job was done and the nurses took over the responsibility for the rest of their patient's care. Mae found some satisfaction in him stumbling over her name, and suspected that he'd found the circumstances more difficult than usual too.

'Just doing my job.' Her slightly quivering voice and bottom lip weren't in keeping with the self-assured comment. At times it was much more than a job, it was a reminder of her own vulnerabilities, and today especially had been something of a wake-up call.

However, she didn't intend to make a show

of herself by crying in front of the team. Apart from Liam, they wouldn't understand why she'd get so emotional over a random patient. It wouldn't look good or do anything for her reputation at her new place of work if they thought she couldn't cope with any vulnerable cases. So she turned on her heel and walked away, not looking back, hoping she'd at least managed to portray someone in charge of her emotions.

Liam could see Mae was upset even if she'd acted professionally and efficiently with him to get their patient back. He checked with the rest of the team that they had everything in place for Anne Marie before he ducked out for a few minutes.

'Mae,' he called down the corridor, jogging towards her. She could have pretended not to hear him, so he appreciated that she waited for him, though he supposed it was only out of propriety rather than a favour to him. She couldn't very well refuse his company for a few moments without people sensing there was something going on and jumping to conclusions.

They walked in silence out of the department and down the dimly lit corridor in the old part of the hospital which afforded them a little privacy. Liam pulled her aside under a staircase, away from prying eyes and listening ears.

'Are you okay?' The question which had been hovering on his lips since she'd left A&E finally burst from his mouth.

Mae nodded, her wide, glistening eyes and chewed bottom lip saying otherwise.

'You can talk to me. I'm not going to make any judgement because you got upset over a vulnerable, young patient. You're only human, Mae.' He wanted to reach out to her, to give her a hug and offer some comfort, but he didn't want to overstep the mark...again.

She swallowed hard and he could see the effort it was taking her not to cry. As much as he wanted to tell her it was okay to show emotion, Liam knew Mae was too proud to be seen so vulnerable at work.

'Knowing Anne Marie was in so much

pain that she thought ending her life was the only option available triggered a lot for me. I'll be okay…don't worry.'

Liam dismissed her attempt to fob him off. It was obvious she was in pain too. 'I've been there too, after Clodagh. We all have our dark days. What's important is that we pick ourselves up again, eventually, and move on. Hopefully Anne Marie will be able to do the same once she realises nothing is worth ending a life for.'

'But have we moved on, Liam? Yes, we're getting up, going to work and acting like normal human beings, but we're still holding back from being with anyone else. Instead of protecting our hearts, aren't we punishing ourselves by holding back?'

Liam smiled. 'Isn't that what I've been saying? I don't want to be alone for ever, and yes, we run the risk of getting hurt again. But if we don't even try…'

'I know. I'm beginning to realise that I still deserve a love life. I don't want to end up sad and lonely, thinking that's all there is for me.'

'Having someone who thinks you're beautiful and amazing does not necessarily mean he's going to hurt you. I kissed you because I like you, because I think we could have something special together.'

He was about to apologise for getting things so very wrong when Mae got there first.

'I'm sorry I didn't answer your messages. I just… Last night was very confusing for me.'

'I get that. It sort of crept up on us both then completely consumed us.' Even now, the passion which had swept them away was bubbling back up to the surface now that he was so close to her again.

'When I had time to mull things over, consider your proposal, I thought perhaps it was short-changing us both. That we were worth more than a purely physical relationship and we'd only be doing it because our exes had battered our confidence.'

'And now?' The hesitation he saw in her eyes, and the fact she hadn't tried to move away from him, led him to believe she might just have had a change of heart.

'Seeing Anne Marie, what she was prepared to do, to give up… We all deserve better. I don't need any more heartache, or another man to throw my life away on, but I'm not dead yet.'

'And I don't have room in my life for anything serious that will take my attention from my daughter. But we both have needs.' At least they were on that page together.

Mae inched closer and danced her fingertips along the buttons on his shirt, making his skin burn without even touching him. 'But I think you were right about what you said last night—we deserve to have a little fun. Neither Diarmuid or Clodagh are going to rule the rest of our lives. Choosing how we do this is our route to freedom.'

Liam liked this decisive Mae, and not just because she was giving him what he wanted. She was taking control of the situation, of her life. He didn't mind, when the whole thing had been his idea in the first place and he'd certainly be reaping the benefits if she agreed to be with him for any amount of time.

'So, really, sleeping together is our first step to independence.' Liam nuzzled into her neck, luxuriating in the scent of vanilla and summer berries clinging to her skin. The pulse in her throat beat hard against his lips and he knew she was as turned on as he was already.

'Uh-huh. Really, we're doing each other a favour...' She gasped as he slid his hand beneath her shirt to touch the bare skin of her back.

'And I do like to be helpful.'

'I have noticed this about you. One good turn deserves another and all that.' She took him by surprise then, kissing him hard on the lips, tangling her fingers in his hair and bringing every nerve end to attention.

The buzz of her pager which eventually broke through their erotic haze to remind them where they were.

'Sorry. I have an appointment to get to,' she said with a grimace.

Liam reached out to trace the smudged lipstick around her lips. 'You might want to redo your make-up beforehand.'

There was that rosy glow in her cheeks again. 'I might just do that.'

She went to walk away, then stopped and turned back. 'So, how are we going to do this?'

They needed a plan about how they would actually get the time alone needed for this secret fling. Even a casual arrangement required some planning when he had to juggle his job, his daughter and dog-sitting an Irish wolfhound.

At least he had tonight covered.

'Mum and Dad promised Shannon she could sleep over later.'

The smile on Mae's face at that news gave him a warm glow inside, knowing he'd been the one to put it there. He hoped by the end of the night she'd be grinning from ear to ear.

'You are sexy. You are wanted. You are fierce. You are an independent woman who does not need a man in her life for anything other than sex. You do not need to see him as anything other than a sex object. You are not, under any circumstances, to fall for him,' Mae told the woman in the mirror with a wag of her finger, but she doubted even the stern look was enough to convince her of any of that.

Well, maybe the being wanted part. Liam had made it pretty clear he was physically attracted to her even if he didn't want any emotional entanglements—which, she reminded herself, was something she needed to avoid too.

She'd spent all last night and most of today vacillating about whether or not she should take this leap into sexual freedom with Liam. That was what it would be for her. An affair free from the emotional restraints of a relationship. She wasn't even sure she was ready for that. But after the way Liam had kissed her, the way she'd felt today when they'd been alone, she was willing to try.

Even now she shivered with the anticipation of what the night had in store. She was standing in her underwear, still deciding what to wear. She lifted the body-skimming polka-dot wiggle dress and held it against her body, then dismissed it. It was sexy, but she worried it would look like she was trying too hard when this was supposed to be a casual hook-up. Now she re-thought the red lacy lingerie in case it looked too obvious, too desperate— too 'my fiancé jilted me and I need someone to find me attractive so I can feel good about myself'. But she remembered this was just about sex, so there was no need for subtlety.

The doorbell rang and she grabbed her second-choice outfit from the bed—a white boho dress with flowers, which she couldn't have worn out in the Irish March weather, but which hopefully showed enough leg to capture Liam's interest.

One last swipe of lip gloss, a quick tidy of the bedroom and she padded downstairs barefoot to answer the door. A deep breath, shaky release and she came face to face with the man who'd been stalking her every thought recently.

'Hi.' That grin was enough to make her believe she'd done the right thing by taking the risk with this crazy scheme.

'Hey, you. Come in.' Mae peered outside to see if anyone had witnessed his arrival. Although she barely knew anyone in the street, she had a feeling that everyone was watching, knowing she was about to embark on a scandalous sex fest…hopefully.

He side-stepped into the hall, one hand behind his back, seemingly feeling as awkward about this as she was. She took comfort in the fact he obviously didn't make a habit of this sort of thing. It was apparent he hadn't been with anyone since Clodagh, but that didn't mean he hadn't been a playboy in his youth.

'Is everything okay, Liam?'

'Yeah, sure.'

'It's just, you're acting kind of weird. If you've changed your mind…' The thought that he might be trying to find a way to let her down gently hit her hard, deflating her ego immediately. It told her just how much she'd been looking forward to being with him when the disappointment settled into her very bones.

He suddenly thrust forward a bunch of flowers. 'I bought these on the way over, then I thought it might seem a bit much, since this isn't really a date. I didn't want you to read too much into it and think I was trying to turn this into something more already. I just thought I should bring you a gift.'

'Thank you. They're beautiful.' Sheer relief made her want to laugh but she bit her lip, not wishing to offend him. It was a sweet gesture—yes, totally unnecessary, but it proved that he wasn't used to this any more than she was.

'So are you.'

Her heart melted at the whole first-date vibe that was going on, expectation thrumming between them as they skirted around the reason he was here.

'I'll just go and put them in some water.' She needed some too, her mouth suddenly dry, the tension becoming too intense to bear in the cramped entrance hall.

'You've got a nice place here. Not too far from the hospital,' he said, following her to the kitchen.

'Yes, I like it.' The conversation was weirdly formal and stilted, so unlike their usual verbal encounters. Discussing their commute to work wasn't in keeping with the idea that this was going to be fun and exciting. A passionate fling, to her mind, shouldn't involve small talk and gifts: it was supposed to be ripping one another's clothes off, too busy kissing to waste time speaking.

She stood at the sink to fill the vase, wondering if this had been a good idea. If it turned into a disaster it would only make things worse. It was supposed to be an ego boost to make them feel better about themselves after being dumped. An awkward, unsatisfactory fumble wasn't going to help her move on. If anything, it would put her off getting involved in any capacity with another man.

She poured herself a glass of water and sighed as she took a sip. The fantasy had been nice while it had lasted. Before Mae had a chance to voice her second thoughts, Liam came to stand behind her, slipping his arms around her waist.

'I've been waiting all day for this,' he whispered into her ear, melting any concerns that this wasn't going to live up to her expectations. His breath against her neck brought her body back to full attention, as though it had been waiting just for him.

As her heart kicked into overdrive, her nipples tightened and arousal burst through the dam walls, she knew she needed Liam.

'Me too.' She could hardly speak, her body entirely focused on Liam's touch—including her brain.

He kissed her neck where the hairs were already standing to attention, her body hyper-aware of him being so close. A soft sigh escaped her lips, which she soon caught again with an intake of breath when he slid his hands under her dress. Skin on skin, he travelled up her thighs, slowly, carefully and confidently. He paused when he reached her panties and she held her breath, waiting to see what he would do next. Much to her dismay he didn't rip them off and toss them aside, but kept skimming the sides of her body until he reached her chest. He pressed himself closer so she could feel how turned on he was, his hardness nestled against her backside. She didn't think she'd ever been so aroused when still fully clothed.

Then he yanked down her bra and the front of her dress, exposing her breasts to the cool air and his strong hands. Her entire being was straining now for his attention, that aching need taking her over completely. When he cupped her breasts and tugged her nipples, she almost orgasmed right there and then.

Unable to remain passive, Mae spun around to kiss him. She began to pull at his T-shirt, desperate to expose his body too, but she had to give up on her quest when he refused to relinquish his quest to drive her insane. He lowered his head and caught her nipple in his mouth, sucking as he kneaded her breasts with both hands. Mae braced herself against the kitchen work top because her legs had apparently stopped working.

He licked, sucked and played with her until she was begging him to give her some release. 'Liam, please…'

She didn't have to ask again. Without hesitation, he put his hands up her dress and whipped her underwear down her legs. Mae was so wet by then, his fingers slid easily inside her. She had to cling on to him for support now that he was totally in control of what was happening to her body. He literally had her at his fingertips. Slow strokes, quick circles and his steady persistence brought her hurtling to release. Liam maintained eye contact as she climaxed, making it all the more intense.

It surprised her, overwhelmed her, as she came again and again. Only when every tremor had finished rippling through her body did he finally release her.

'Are you okay?' he asked softly.

'Uh-huh.' She didn't even know what words were any more.

Liam grinned. 'I'll take that as a yes. You want to take this upstairs?'

She nodded, though even that took effort. Her body no longer felt like hers, more like a marionette manipulated by Liam, and without him she didn't know how to move any more. He took her hand, but they'd only taken a couple of steps when her knees buckled and she had to grab hold of him to remain upright.

'Although I'm not sure if I can.' She was no virgin and, though it had been a while, she still remembered every lover she'd ever had. None had had this effect on her, making her orgasm so hard, so quickly, it left her incapacitated. Especially when they hadn't even slept together. If this was just a taste of the power he could have over, how they could be together, Mae already knew she wouldn't want this to end between them.

That definitely wasn't in keeping with their casual agreement.

Liam caught her before she fell and swept her up in his arms, ignoring her protests that she was too heavy. 'Sure, there's nothing of you.'

To prove his point, he carried her straight upstairs with a swagger to his step, which might have been caused by the pride of bringing Mae to climax so easily, or by the erection pressing against his fly as she nuzzled into his chest. Either way, the encounter had bolstered him mentally and physically and he couldn't wait for more. As long as Mae was up to it.

She seemed wiped out. He supposed it was a lot to process after being on her own for such a long time. He could only imagine how he was going to feel after the same, not that it was making his jeans any more comfortable. The last people they'd slept with were people they'd been in relationships with, partners they'd loved and who'd ultimately found them lacking in some way. This might only be a sexual release for both of them now, but that didn't mean there wouldn't be some emotional involvement. If not with each other, at least for themselves. They needed it—to know they were normal, they were wanted and that they were able to move on from their pasts.

'That one.' Mae pointed towards the door at the end of the landing.

He nudged it open, taking her into a room filled with photos and trinkets of her life in Boston, a little nest of comfort she'd built for herself in this new country. The fact that she was giving him permission to enter into this sanctuary showed how much trust she was putting in him not to hurt her—another reason this couldn't go beyond a non-meaningful fling. Mae deserved someone who would put her feelings above everyone else's, and he couldn't prioritise her over Shannon. All he could do was make her feel good, make her feel appreciated and wanted, for as long as they had together.

He set her down on the mattress, nestled in the bank of cushions adorning the bed. With an impatient swipe of her hands, Mae nudged them onto the floor, then proceeded to strip her dress over her head. She tossed it on the floor with her bra, so she was lying there beautifully naked waiting for him, the red hair spread around her making her look like Venus come to life.

Liam had a sudden moment of imposter syndrome, believing he wasn't worthy of being here with her. That he was as bad as her ex, using her to satiate his needs without considering her feelings enough. Those negative thoughts only lasted until she hooked her fingers into the belt loops on his jeans and pulled him closer.

'Aren't you going to join me?' Despite her bravado, he could see her nervously worrying her bottom lip with her teeth and realised she needed this as much as he did.

'If you insist.' As eager as he was to get naked with her, he took his time undressing, watching the appreciation and desire turn her eyes to glittering jade. The T-shirt went first, joining the pile of clothes and cushions on the floor. He reached for her hand and moved it over his chest, down his stomach and briefly over his crotch.

'I like it when you touch me.' His honesty manifested itself almost as a growl, his voice so thick with arousal and lust for her.

Mae sat up, alert once more, the weariness dissipating as she took her cue. Kneeling on the bed, she unbuckled his belt, every deliberate movement extending the foreplay. When she popped open the buttons on his fly, it was all he could do to restrain himself, but he wasn't going to rush the best thing to happen to him in months. Instead, he stood tall, clinging on to his resolve as she pushed his jeans away and teased his erection through his boxers. She gripped him through the cotton fabric and he gritted his teeth together, fighting every natural urge that came rushing forward at her touch.

When she pulled his underwear down and exclaimed, 'Well, hello, soldier!', all bets were off. He loved this playful, flirtatious side to Mae. Along with her touch, it helped him forget about everything his ex had done to him and simply enjoy the moment with her.

In a hurry to kick off the rest of his clothes, he almost stumbled onto the bed with her, spurred on by her little giggle. Lying face to face, Liam kissed her, luxuriating in the soft, welcoming feel of her lips against his. She'd become his sanctuary.

Something between them seemed to have shifted in those few seconds. The frenzied passion was now a sensual exploration as they caressed each other's naked bodies, the kisses tender and softer than before, as if they were drawing comfort from one another rather than embarking on what was supposed to be a wild, reckless shag-a-thon.

Mae must have thought the same, as her gentle strokes along his shaft now became insistent and demanding, until he couldn't think straight, forcing all his energy into not embarrassing himself, and also wanting her with a hunger that was eating him from the inside out.

He moved so she was underneath him, her soft breasts pushed so temptingly against him he couldn't resist, especially when she was so responsive every time he touched her there. With one breast cupped in his palm, he grazed his teeth over the sensitive bud atop, tugging on it until she was groaning and writhing with a mixture of frustration and pleasure. He knew, because he felt it too. He was enjoying all the sensations, wanting instant gratification but also wanting to make this last for ever. The horny excitement, the restlessness and stimulation of being together and not yet consummating their relationship, were all preferable to feeling miserable, analysing where he'd gone wrong and worrying about the future.

Mae liked him, and clearly wanted him, and that was enough for now. She grabbed his backside and pulled him flush against her—a woman who knew her own mind and wasn't afraid to show him what was on it.

'I need to get some protection.' He'd bought a packet of condoms in preparation and, though he was loath to move from his current position, they were lying in the heap of clothes on the floor.

'In my night stand. Hold on.' Mae rummaged one-handed in the drawer beside the bed and produced a foil packet.

He raised an eyebrow. 'I don't mean to be judgemental, but I was under the impression you hadn't been with anyone since... you know.'

He hated himself for even thinking it, never mind saying it. It was none of his business if she'd been in bed with half the country, but he found himself irrationally hating anyone who'd been here with her before him. Part of the reason he'd bonded with Mae was that they'd been in similar circumstances relationship-wise and, to him, that included post-break-up celibacy, so they'd experience this breakthrough in their emotional and physical development together.

Ugh. So much for 'no strings' if he was jealous of anyone she potentially could have slept with before they'd even met.

'Sorry. Sorry. I have no right to say anything about your love life.'

Mae held his face in her hands and locked her eyes on to his. 'I haven't been with anyone since my non-wedding day. I haven't wanted to be with anyone until you. And I haven't any intention of sleeping with anyone but you for the near future, okay? I bought them especially. I mean, if we're embarking on some sort of sex-fest until we're both rendered incapable of walking and talking, we don't want to run out, right?'

'Right. I'm sorry…'

Mae placed a finger on his lips. 'No apologies. Just fun.'

'Just fun,' he muttered against her finger before drawing it into his mouth and sucking it hard.

Mae continued the battle of one-upmanship by putting the condom on him herself, Liam breaking out in a sweat as he fought so hard to maintain his composure.

'You do not play fair at all, Dr Watters.' Pinning her hands to the bed, he kissed the smug smile of satisfaction from her lips.

He nudged her knees apart and positioned himself between her legs, entering her in one swift move that seemed to stun them both. It certainly took him a long, hot minute to recompose himself, once the fireworks had stopped going off in his head. Mae's little gasp when he entered her soon turned to a sigh of satisfaction as he moved inside her. Every time they joined together was a test of his restraint when he just wanted to give himself over to the euphoria he was experiencing. Dipping in and out of her felt like a new reward every time.

Greedy for more, he hooked her legs over his shoulders and pushed deeper, harder, faster. Mae's gasps became louder, quicker, more ragged. Then he realised his breathing was rapid too, that pressure to give in to his release becoming so intense, he thought he'd explode.

He watched where their bodies were joined as he slid in and out of this beautiful woman, realising how privileged he was to be in this position. To be with Mae. He kissed her, long and passionately, showing her how grateful he was with every thrust of his hips. He waited until she tightened around him, clutching at his back as her orgasm hit, until he found complete satisfaction too. Mae's cry was drowned out by his roar of triumph, their bodies rocking together until they had nothing left to give and his throat was raw.

Yet he found himself reluctant to move away when it was all over, only doing so when his knees were too weak to hold him up any longer.

'This might just kill me,' he said, rolling over beside her.

'Yeah, but you'll die happy.' Mae turned on her side and kissed him.

'Amen.' He lay on his back, fighting to get his breath back and praying this wouldn't be the last time they had this. That it was only the beginning. He needed this feeling, needed Mae, to help him forget all the bad stuff and, yes, make him happy. It was a long time since he'd had anything in his life to smile about and now it would be hard to wipe the grin off his face.

'What are you smiling about?'

'This. You, and how you make me feel like a king,' he said honestly. There was no point in hiding it, not when communication had been his downfall in the past and he wanted this to last with Mae for as long as possible.

'I think you did all the hard work…this time.' Mae stood up and walked towards the bathroom, giving him an envious view of her pert backside. Though he was sorry she was leaving him in bed without her, he kept hold of her words, the twinkle in her eye and the promise that they would do this all over again.

CHAPTER SEVEN

MAE STARED AT the reflection in the bathroom mirror. She didn't recognise the flushed face staring back or the twinkle back in her eyes, and her hair made her look as though she'd been thoroughly ravished in bed. Which she had. The wanton woman smiled back at her. This was exactly what she needed: fun; an ego boost… Liam.

And it felt safe, knowing he couldn't break her heart, because she wasn't going to give it to him. He could have her body; she'd give it willingly after he'd showed her exactly what he could do with it. The rest she intended to keep under lock and key, knowing she couldn't trust anyone not to damage it—including herself.

That said, she wasn't in a rush for their

tryst to end just yet. She splashed some water over her face and freshened up before going back into the room. The sight of Liam stretched out naked on her bed convinced her that, just because this was supposed to be casual, it didn't mean he shouldn't stay a little while longer. Since Shannon was staying at his parents' place, and he didn't seem to be in a hurry to leave either, Mae slid back into bed next to him.

'No taxi waiting for you?'

'No…sorry, do you want me to leave?' He sat up immediately and reached down for his clothes, clearly mistaking her teasing for a hint he should leave.

'No. Not at all. I just thought that might be how these things work—you know?—wham, bam.'

'There was no "wham bam" involved, but I do thank you, ma'am—very, very much.' Liam punctuated the words with kisses dotted along her collarbone, making her feel she never wanted him to leave.

'I just… I don't do this. I guess I'm just trying to figure out what the rules are.' She didn't want to misstep and have it end when she was already enjoying the benefits.

'We make our own rules. If we want to cuddle after, hey, that's normal—I think. As long as we're both comfortable with what's happening, I don't see any reason to bolt the second the deed is done.'

'The deed?' She chuckled.

'You know what I mean. We're only here for one thing.' He let his hand drift along the curve of her waist, barely touching her, but her body responded all the same, ready to accept him all over again.

'Yeah, but there's no rush, is there? Shannon's with your mum and dad, and it seems foolish for us both to spend the night alone in separate houses. Not that I'm expecting you to stay over, or anything. But, you know, we can hang out, order takeaway and watch trash TV. If that doesn't seem too much like breaking the rules?' She didn't want to frighten him off but it would be nice to have some company. Since moving in, she'd spent every night on her own, and it seemed a little churlish to send him home simply because it breached the 'hook-up and done' code.

'Look.' He turned onto his side, giving her a serious look. 'We both know the score. Neither of us is going to read more into what's happening than what we've agreed to. I'd actually enjoy doing something normal, like ordering some food and vegging out in front of the telly. In company, for once. No, this probably isn't like any other casual relationship because we already know each other, and we work together. As long as we are both happy, I don't see the problem. If that changes, then we'll reconsider our arrangement. Deal?'

'Deal.' Mae shook his outstretched hand. It didn't seem odd at all to make a deal whilst lying naked with a co-worker, the way her life had been going lately. Infinitely preferable to moving halfway across the world and being dumped on her wedding day.

'Okay, so… Chinese, Indian, burgers…?' Liam lifted his phone and began scrolling.

'Chinese,' she said without hesitation, her stomach rumbling, having been too nervous to eat anything before their date.

He held the screen so she could see the menu and pick what she wanted to eat, then he added his order, along with extra portions of rice and noodles. 'Done.'

When Mae saw the size of the order he'd just put in, she began to get concerned. 'The way you've been feeding me recently, I'm going to end up the size of a house.'

She'd already put on a little weight on after the wedding, during her comfort eating stage.

'I like your curves,' he said, grabbing hold of her backside and pulling her flush against him. 'Besides, we can always work off a few calories.'

'Yeah?' With his eyes darkening with desire, it was clear how he planned to work out. His idea of exercise sure beat those dreaded early-morning gym trips. She might just cancel her membership and employ him as her personal trainer instead.

'Well, the app says delivery is going to take at least an hour. I think we could squeeze in a good workout, you know? Build up an appetite.' He was moving over her again, covering her with his body and rolling her onto her back. Mae submitted completely and willingly.

'We wouldn't want to get lazy. It's important to balance diet and exercise for your well-being,' she muttered as he dipped his head to capture her mouth once more.

Mae sighed into the kiss, reaching up to wind her fingers in Liam's hair and claim him as hers for a little while longer. This was all temporary—a fantasy she was allowed to indulge in to make her feel better about herself. It was working. When she was with Liam, he treated her like a goddess. She was no longer the rejected bride not worthy of love but a sexy, confident single woman embarking on a passionate fling. Liam O'Conner was just the tonic she needed.

'You want another beer?' Mae shouted from the kitchen.

'Why not? I can always walk home.' Whilst he had no intention of going to work with a hangover tomorrow, he was enjoying the evening.

Eating a takeaway while watching soap

operas was a normal night. Liam did it all the time. So why did it feel so special just because he was doing it with Mae? Probably because it felt comfortable, knowing she was happy to do it. Even on the nights he and Clodagh had been at home together, she hadn't wanted to sit in with him, preferring to go out with 'the girls'. He'd been too boring, too staid, because he'd simply wanted family time together. Secrecy was a big part of his arrangement with Mae, for everyone's sake. It also meant there wasn't any pressure to go out clubbing, or try to be someone he wasn't. This was enough for her, and so was he.

'There's enough food left to feed the street.' She tossed him a beer and curled up beside him on the sofa.

'We can box it up and put it in the fridge once it's cooled down. I'll have it for breakfast.'

'Yuk.' She screwed up her nose and took a slug of beer from her bottle. 'I don't know how you can eat so much and still look so good.'

'I do have to work at it. I've got a home

gym, and eat salads in between parent visits usually. I've made an exception for you this week, but it's nice to know you think I'm hot.' He was teasing her but she was definitely giving him an ego boost. Not only with her comments, but the way she'd responded to him in bed, where he knew he was most definitely doing something right.

Liam supposed sex had kind of taken a back seat between Clodagh and him due to shift clashes and, if he was honest, a lack of interest. They hadn't made enough time, or effort. Yet he seemed to be able to find both for Mae. Perhaps he'd known deep down that he and Clodagh were over and had checked out long before she had.

In which case, he couldn't blame her for having gone elsewhere. It was being with Mae that showed him all that had been missing in the relationship—passion, fun and enjoying one another. He'd settled for less because he wanted to save his family, provide some stability in Shannon's life and be the good parent he'd had growing up, but family life had been far from perfect. Some day he hoped he could have it all: a romantic, fun relationship that also nurtured a loving environment for his daughter to grow up in.

'You know you are. Confidence is not something you seem to have a problem with.'

'A common misconception about me. Yes, I'm an extrovert, but that doesn't mean I don't have hang-ups like everyone else. You know how it feels when you've been rejected—it hurts.'

He saw her wince and mentally kicked himself for bringing up her past relationship woes and spoiling the evening. 'Sorry. I just mean we're here together tonight because we're too afraid to commit to a proper relationship again. This is safe until we're ready to trust someone with our hearts some day.'

Mae scrambled to sit upright, her legs tucked under her to bring her up to the same height as Liam. 'So you think you'll want to do the whole serious relationship again? That's not for me.'

'No? Never, ever?' He let out a long breath. 'I don't think I could do that. I need to be with someone.'

'Why is it so important? You're doing okay, just you and Shannon. Why do you need to bring a third party in to make you happy, knowing they could do the opposite?'

He had to think on that one for a bit, knowing her fears were justified. It wasn't that he hadn't considered it: it was why they were keeping this secret, after all. He didn't want Shannon to get hurt, and by keeping things casual with Mae he was protecting his own heart. Especially knowing she didn't want another serious relationship. Ultimately, though, he thought the risk would be worth taking if he could still find that special someone to share his life with.

'I know a lot of people resent their parents, or choose partners that are the complete opposite to who they were, but you've met my mum and dad. They're great, right?'

She nodded with a smile. 'Yes, they are.'

'Growing up in that place was the happiest time of my life. I know it's unconventional, and it was noisy, and they were always working, but they always made time for me and each other. Family was the most important thing, and I still believe that. I just want that sort of security for Shannon, as well as for me. I know she has me and her grandparents, even her mother on occasion, but it's not the same. I want someone to share the parenting with, to cook dinner with after work, to go on holiday and make plans for the future with. Maybe even have more kids some day. I don't want one failed relationship to take all of that away for ever.'

Mae watched him with something he was sure was a mixture of surprise and sadness. As though she didn't believe he could still want all of that, and sure she was too afraid to.

'I can sort of see where you're coming from, even if my childhood has given me a different perspective on that. I never knew my father: he split when I was little, leaving Mum to raise me. I loved her so much. She was like my best friend, you know? So strong and independent and caring. Losing her... Well, it was devastating.' Her voice faltered. 'I tried the serious relationship thing with Diarmuid, but in hindsight I think I was just looking for a replacement—something to fill the void the loss of my mother had created. I realise now I'm not going to find that with anyone. She's simply irreplaceable.'

Liam saw through her smile to the heartbreak and loneliness inside her. At least he had Shannon and his parents to keep him buoyed, and remind him he was loved. Mae had no one and it was a shame she wanted to keep it that way.

'By your own admission, your marriage was probably a mistake. Something you rushed into. That doesn't mean there isn't someone out there who's perfect for you, that you could be happy with. Didn't you ever want a family of your own?'

It was a simple enough question, but it packed a powerful punch straight through Mae's defences and straight to her heart. Liam *saw* her.

'I did, at one point. I mean, when you grow up in a one-parent family always struggling for money, it's the dream to have the whole family package, including a dad to love and support you. When I met Diarmuid, I thought we would have that too. I guess it was better he left me when he did, rather than walk away later on an entire family. It's made me think about what a lucky escape I've had and how careful I need to be in future. I don't want to inflict a difficult childhood on an innocent child because I got carried away in a romantic fantasy.

'The reality of life is that relationships don't work out. I've accepted that. I mean, if you'd known Clodagh was going to leave, would you have started a family?' Mae threw the question back at him even though she knew she was treading on dangerous ground, because Shannon was everything to Liam. She just wanted him to realise the gravity behind her making that kind of decision—choosing to protect potential offspring before they even came into existence.

The uncharacteristic scowl suggested perhaps she had strayed too far beyond those blurred lines between a fling and something more personal. She doubted a no-strings arrangement included deep and meaningful conversations about their life choices and motivations.

'We can't live our lives on "ifs" and "buts", Mae, or we'd never accomplish anything. Okay, so it didn't work out between Clodagh and I, but I wouldn't be without Shannon. Would I have done things differently given a chance? Yes. Perhaps I was more invested in the idea of family than putting in the work to make sure we stayed together, but I don't regret becoming a father. I regret letting her and Clodagh down by not doing enough to make the relationship work, but I'm not going to let it steal my future from me. I've learned some lessons, and hope it will help me if I do ever get into another long-term relationship, but there's no point in looking back any more. Being with you has shown me that.' He grabbed hold of her feet and pulled her, so she slid down the couch towards him, and kissed her.

Mae's eyes fluttered shut and she let the feel of his lips dictate her mood instead of the noise currently buzzing in her head. She wanted to focus on Liam kissing her, on being together right now, instead of worrying about the future.

Except she couldn't put his words to the back of her mind just yet. He still wanted marriage, a family and everything she'd thought was possible once upon a time. She wished she had his optimism, or even that she could be 'the one' for him and that they'd all live happily ever after. Life had cruelly illustrated to her that it wasn't a realistic expectation, even if Liam did make a good argument.

Fear held her back from being with someone. From being with Liam. She was scared of being rejected again, of her heart taking another beating, of planning a future together and having it whipped away from her again. The only thing worse than having to go through that again, of losing someone else she loved, would be having a child live through it too. She wouldn't be able to live with the guilt of that. Yet the way Liam talked about his daughter, the love he obviously had for her, made her heart ache a little more. It was as though she'd lost an entire family because of Diarmuid, because she could never let anyone get close to her again after the way he'd treated her.

In moments like this, being with Liam, she was beginning to have second thoughts about remaining alone. 'For ever' seemed like a long time, especially if it meant not having company like this, with someone who knew her. What she had with Liam wasn't something she'd be able to replicate in the future. A casual fling with some random guy she met in a bar or club was never going to have the same depth as this thing with Liam. She knew that after only one day. This wasn't just sex, it was amazing sex, and she wondered if that was because they knew more about each other than two strangers who'd simply hooked up one night.

The passion and desire had likely built up from seeing each other at work and not being able to touch one another. She wondered if that was sustainable. It certainly felt like it, when they were already pulling at each other's clothes again, impatient to experience that ecstasy together all over again.

More frighteningly, perhaps she was beginning to ask herself if this could be more than stealing a few hours together. Liam had been open about wanting a partner willing to settle down and raise a family with him and, whilst Mae didn't know if she was open to that possibility, she had definitely grown close to Liam and his daughter.

The question now was whether or not she was willing to risk her peace of mind for more time with Liam.

Liam was wrapped around Mae's naked body, trying to get his breath back—again. This time they hadn't made it to the bedroom and, despite the uncomfortable confines of the sofa, his body was finally getting weary. He was in danger of falling into a food and sex coma, having over-indulged in both. Not that he was complaining. He just needed a little time before he was ready for action again.

'I should probably go,' he muttered into the back of her neck as they lay spooning on the couch.

Mae groaned and wriggled against him,

not doing anything to persuade him he should leave.

'We both need some sleep.' He half-heartedly tried again to convince them both to move, but he was pleasantly exhausted, and quite happy to remain in situ with Mae in his arms.

'You could stay. I mean, it's too late to walk home, if you could even manage to stand right now, and it seems pointless paying for a taxi when your car's outside...'

'I don't know...'

'I just thought, you know, if you wanted to stay on the couch for the night. Sorry... I didn't mean to over-step any boundaries.' Mae sat up, extracting herself from his arms and grabbing the clothes she'd discarded earlier.

'Hey. I know you were only thinking of me. Don't worry. It's just that I don't have a toothbrush and I don't want to spoil the illusion of this erotic fantasy with my very real morning breath.'

Liam didn't want her to feel bad because he hadn't immediately jumped at her invitation. He'd hesitated because it had crossed his mind that staying the night wasn't in keeping with the idea of 'just sex', but he supposed they'd crossed that line some time ago. Having dinner and discussing their past relationships over drinks probably wasn't the norm for this kind of set-up.

It wasn't that he didn't want to stay the night: it would be easier, and it would mean he didn't have to go home to an empty house. He was merely worried that staying over with Mae might become too comfortable. This felt more like the beginning of a relationship than something that wasn't supposed to have any emotional attachment for them. He already knew he had feelings for Mae that went beyond the physical—a bad move when she'd told him in no uncertain terms she didn't want a commitment.

Yet, they were electric together, and that wasn't something he could easily walk away from. Especially when his legs were like jelly after all his exertions tonight.

'I'm sure I have a spare in the bathroom.

If you want to stay…if it's not breaking the rules…'

'I'm not going to stay on the sofa, Mae.'

'Oh. Okay. Do you need me to order a cab?' She looked a little crestfallen and Liam almost felt bad about teasing her.

'If I'm sleeping here tonight, I want to do it in your bed. These bones of mine are getting too old to spend the night anywhere but in a nice, comfy bed.' That definitely wasn't in keeping with the idea of just sex, but they'd already crossed so many boundaries that others might consider casual that it hardly mattered now. Not if it meant waking up in Mae's arms. Who knew when they'd next get to spend time together, never mind an entire night? Liam intended to make the most of his child-free time.

Although Mae was smiling, seemingly pleased by his decision, he did sense some hesitation before she took it when he held out his hand to her.

'I only meant to sleep. I don't believe you can have too much of a good thing, but I do think some recovery time is necessary before you indulge again.' Liam grinned, fully intending to indulge again before he finally had to leave. He knew they were both exhausted, with jobs and lives of their own to go back to tomorrow, but they could let the fantasy go on a little bit longer.

'A sleep, a shower and some breakfast in the morning should set us both to rights again.' Mae led the way back upstairs, with Liam keen to follow.

'That sounds like a plan.' And an excellent way to start a new day. It was a shame this was probably only a one-off when the thought of waking up in Mae's bed, with her naked beside him, was likely something he could easily get used to.

The sound of his phone buzzing roused Liam from a deep sleep. It took him a few seconds to come to in the dark and realise where he was. Then Mae stirred beside him and he was tempted to ignore the call and snuggle back under the sheets with her. Instead, one glance at the screen and he was straight out of bed, phone in hand.

'Dad? What's wrong?' It was three o'clock in the morning and he knew his parents wouldn't have called him unless something was seriously amiss.

'Sorry to wake you, son, but it's Shannon.'

Liam's stomach plummeted through the floor. 'What's happened?'

He bounded down the stairs and grabbed his clothes from the floor, dressing one-handed while waiting to hear whatever bad news his father was about to impart.

'Now, don't panic...'

The very words were guaranteed to make him panic.

'Is she all right?'

'She's had a fall. I'm not sure if she was disoriented in the dark, or if she was sleep walking, but she fell down the stairs. The poor lamb knocked herself out for a bit and I think she might have broken her arm. I've phoned for an ambulance but I thought maybe you could get here quicker to take a look and reassure her.'

He could have, if he hadn't been drinking

at Mae's house, but he didn't want to tell them that and complicate the situation any further.

'I'll be there as quick as I can.' Liam hung up so he could order a taxi, cursing himself for taking his eyes off the ball. In paying more heed to his libido than his daughter, he'd failed her and left her to get hurt whilst he'd been out pretending he was a single man with no responsibilities.

Liam lifted one of his shoes and fired it across the room, watching it ricochet off the kitchen door. A pointless exercise, since he had to go and pick it up again or he couldn't leave the house, and it did nothing to alleviate the guilt and frustration he was experiencing. He was angry at himself for going against everything he'd promised himself and Shannon after Clodagh had left. Spending the night with Mae hadn't been putting his daughter's needs first, and it certainly hadn't been the action of a man trying to be a better father. It had been selfish and foolish, and now his daughter was going to pay the price for his mistakes, again.

'Is there something wrong?' Mae appeared

in the doorway, hair in disarray, eyes half-closed with sleep, tying the belt of her dressing gown around her waist.

Liam clenched his teeth together, trying to ignore the fact that her bare legs seemed to go on for ever and that he knew exactly what was under that robe. 'Shannon fell down the stairs and hurt herself. I have to get to the pub.'

'I'm so sorry. Let me come with you.'

'The taxi's on its way. I'm not waiting for you. My daughter needs me and I've already let her down tonight.'

'I swear I'll be two minutes. Let me help. If I'm not down when the cab comes, you can go without me.' She hovered in the doorway, waiting for him to give her the nod, to let her know things were okay between them.

Although he was regretting leaving Shannon tonight, it wasn't Mae's fault. She'd done everything right. That was the problem. He hadn't wanted to leave, and he knew that was bad news for the future. A fling between them was always going to be complicated and he simply couldn't afford this level of distraction taking him away from his daughter.

He also knew turning up together would cause problems. His parents weren't stupid; they'd know they'd spent the night together. Since he was already having second thoughts about continuing whatever this was with Mae, explaining the circumstances was not going to put him in a good light with anyone. He would need to come up with a pretty good excuse as to why she was with him at this time of the morning if he was to avoid embarrassing everyone involved.

However, if the ambulance was too far away and Shannon had been seriously hurt, he might need an extra pair of medical hands. His daughter's welfare had to come before his personal problems—something he should have remembered before he let her get hurt. Now he would simply have to swallow his pride and get to his daughter as fast as possible. Any difficult conversations to be had with his parents and Mae would have to wait until he knew Shannon was all right.

'Two minutes,' he said gruffly, hoping it expressed both his impatience and a hint that this was already over between them.

Mae raced back upstairs and he opened the door, waiting for the glare of the taxi headlights to turn into the street, part of him hoping it would appear before Mae did, so he didn't have to face the problem of her being there. Mae would understand if he went without her. After all, a single dad called away to deal with his daughter in the middle of the night wasn't the fun he'd promised. It represented the sort of commitment she'd told him she didn't want in her life.

When she did bounce back downstairs ready to go, clad in jeans, sweater and pulling on a pair of running shoes, it prompted him to ask himself why. If Mae was prepared to involve herself in his domestic dramas, it had to be because she was more invested in Shannon and him than she'd even realised. Whilst ultimately that was what he wanted, someone who'd be there for Shannon and him, he knew that wasn't the future Mae saw for herself.

There was no point in fooling themselves that this was going to work. It wouldn't be fair to anyone when it inevitably ended, no one satisfied with what they'd settled for.

They would have to put this down to what it was—a one-night stand with added complications—and go back to their own separate lives. It had been nice while it lasted, a brief respite from beating himself up over his personal failures. Once he was assured Shannon was okay, it would be back to business as usual.

The cab ride over to the pub was excruciating. Liam hadn't spoken to her since they'd left the house and she knew it was because he regretted everything that had happened between them. If they hadn't been so caught up in one another, Liam would have been at home with Shannon and she wouldn't have hurt herself. For someone who'd been so careful to protect his daughter until now, he'd be devastated by these events.

Mae could have let him go to deal with the situation himself, but she'd feared if she did she might never see him again, at least outside of a professional capacity. She still wasn't ready for their time to end just yet and hoped by showing him she cared about Shannon too they might be able to salvage something between them.

Although she'd sworn not to commit to anything or anyone capable of breaking her heart somewhere down the line, she was already in too deep with Liam to walk away now. If they couldn't manage to keep things casual, she hoped they could at least take things slowly if she was to venture back into a relationship.

Talking tonight, enjoying each other's company, making love and going to bed together at the end of the day were all things she'd been missing in her life. Liam had shown her what she could still have if she was brave enough to open up her life, and her heart, to the possibility of being with someone again.

Yes, it was scary embarking on something with a man who had such a great responsibility as a father but, if being a part of his family was what it took for him to continue seeing one another, Mae was willing to try. As long as they went into it with their eyes open, aware of how they'd both been scarred in the past, and promising never to reopen those old wounds with actions of their own, they might stand a chance.

'Thanks.'

Liam threw some money at the driver outside the pub before getting out of the car without even looking back to see if Mae was following. Obviously his primary concern was for Shannon, but it still hurt she didn't warrant a smidge of his attention.

'She's inside. We thought we'd keep her downstairs so the paramedics could get to her easier.' Paddy met them at the entrance of the dark pub, which seemed so eerie at this time of the morning with no one else around, the noise of customers seemingly a distant memory.

They crossed the rain-soaked cobbles and rushed inside, both praying Shannon wasn't too badly injured.

'The ambulance is on the way. We loaned the car to Sean tonight so he could go to the cash and carry for us in the morning, otherwise we would have driven her ourselves.' They found his mother cradling Shannon in one of the booths in which only a few hours ago people would've been sitting, drinking and having fun.

'It's fine. We're here now. Daddy's here, sweetie.' Liam moved so Shannon was resting her head on his lap instead of his mother's.

Mae saw the look Moira gave Liam and her, but she made no comment and received no explanation, though it must've been obvious what had gone on. She must look a mess with mega bedhead, not to mention her make-up sweated off after her sex session with Liam, wearing the first clothes that came to hand. That alone would've signalled what they'd been up to, even if arriving together in the early hours of the morning hadn't.

She felt herself heat up under Moira's scrutiny and ducked into the other side of the booth from Liam, out of harm's way. 'How is she?'

'There's quite a bad gash at her temple. Is your head hurting, sweetie?' Liam brushed her blood-matted hair away from her face, the look of love in his eyes for his daughter so intense, it made Mae want to weep.

It was a promise to love and protect her at

all costs. Mae had never had any man look at her that way, parent or partner. Nor was she likely to if she didn't open up her life, and her heart, to let someone close enough to love her like that. At this moment in time, she was tempted to go against everything she'd promised herself and take a risk on love again if it meant Liam might look at her like that some day.

'Where were you, Daddy? I had a bad dream and I couldn't find you.'

Mae didn't know which was worse to witness—the little girl's distress, or the cloud of guilt that moved over her father's face. She wanted to reach out and hug both of them, but knew that would be over-stepping so many boundaries in front of Liam's family and he wouldn't appreciate it.

'I know, Shannon. I'm sorry. I'll never leave you on your own again, okay? Now, can you be a big, brave girl and let me see where you're hurt?'

Shannon nodded slowly, naturally wary but trusting her father not to do anything to cause her any unnecessary pain. Liam would blame himself for Shannon getting hurt, of course—that was the nature of a good parent—but it was an accident that no one could have prevented. Mae wasn't ashamed to admit she envied their relationship when it had been missing in her life for too long. She'd never had it with her father and, now that her mother was gone, there was no one in her life she could trust implicitly always to look out for her like that. If she didn't take a few risks, she never would.

'Could you put some more lights on, Paddy, please? And Moira, could you pass me the first-aid kit?' If she was going to be seen here tonight as someone other than the harlot who'd tempted a good dad away from his daughter, then Mae needed to earn her place.

Immediately, Paddy and Moira sprang into action, and she was sure they were simply glad to have a part to play too. Now that they could better see what they were dealing with, Liam helped Shannon on to the table.

Mae began cleaning the wound on the little girl's temple. 'This might sting a little bit,

Shannon, but we have to clean the area to see how deep the cut is.'

'I need to see this arm too, love.' Liam tried to persuade her to let him assess what damage had been done there, but Shannon cradled the limp limb closer to her body, refusing his request.

Once Mae had finished dressing the head wound, she moved around to join Liam at the end of the table to face Shannon. 'You're lucky. You have two doctors who want to help you feel better. Won't you let us take a look? It won't heal unless we do, and you don't want to go about with one wing for ever, do you?'

That made Shannon smile, especially when Liam quacked at her. 'You're my little lame duck, aren't you, Shannon?'

'Quack, quack,' she responded, and tentatively held out her arm for Liam to look at it.

'Good girl.'

Carefully, Liam felt along the bruised arm, Shannon flinching when he reached her elbow. 'Okay, I think there's a fracture there. We need to stabilise that until the paramedics get here. Is there any update on that?'

'I'll phone again.' Paddy disappeared back behind the bar.

'Moira, do you have anything we could use as a splint? Like a piece of wood, or even a rolled-up newspaper would do for now. We could tie that around her arm temporarily to immobilise it.'

Mae wanted to do something other than sit waiting for someone else to help Shannon. She hated to see her in pain, as much as she disliked watching her father's anguish. It was important to her that she could be there for them and Mae realised that she'd already made that commitment she was so afraid of. Once Shannon was treated at the hospital and they knew she was all right, Mae would discuss the matter with Liam. If he was on board, she'd like to take that first step back into the relationship world with him.

'Here you go. I brought a couple of towels too.' Moira returned with some makeshift medical supplies for Mae to use whilst Liam reassured his daughter they were working in her best interests.

'Shannon, if you can hold your arm out,

Mae is going to tie some things around it to keep it straight. We need you to stay still until she's all done.' Liam had one arm around Shannon's waist, holding her close, with the other presenting the broken limb for Mae to work on.

She was grateful he was allowing her to be of some assistance when she knew he was quite capable of doing all this on his own. Hopefully it was a sign that he was ready for her to be part of their lives too.

'When you get to the hospital they'll put a proper cast on it for you, but we're just going to tie this on now so it doesn't hurt any more when you move it.' Mae used the bandages in the first-aid kit to hold the temporary fix in place, but she was relieved when she heard the sirens outside.

'I'll go and direct them in.' Paddy, still in his pyjamas, rushed out into the street so they didn't waste any time trying to locate their patient. A short time later, he returned with two paramedics, carrying their first-aid gear.

'Over here.' Liam waved them over and

Mae moved out of the way so they had full access to examine Shannon.

'It looks as though someone has beat us to it,' one of the men commented on seeing Shannon's home-made splint.

'We're both doctors, but unfortunately we didn't have the means to get her to hospital ourselves tonight. Shannon had a fall down the stairs while she was staying with my parents. She had a bad knock to the head, and was briefly unconscious, but she's responsive and seems fine at the moment.'

'No sickness or dizzy spells?'

'No. She was out cold for a few moments, the longest time of my life. We just didn't want to do anything that might do her more harm than good.' Moira was hovering by the table, understandably concerned with her granddaughter's welfare, and no doubt blaming herself as much as Liam for the accident.

'That's fine. We'll do an X-ray on that arm at the hospital, Shannon, and try and make you more comfortable, but there's nothing to worry about. Is Mum or Dad coming with us in the ambulance?'

'I'm her dad. Mae's just a friend.' Liam asserted his position, and Mae's at the same time, as he scooped Shannon up into his arms, ready to leave.

'I guess I'll phone a cab to take me home.' Despite her role in the drama, Mae was left feeling like a spare part with no real reason to be here, with Liam willing to leave her with his parents in an awkward post-hook-up situation.

'That's probably for the best. I'll call you later.'

The promise to get back in touch was the only thing saving her from total humiliation. It wouldn't do to get too needy; Liam was always going to put his daughter first. He was that kind of man, and if he hadn't been she probably wouldn't even be thinking of venturing into something beyond casual with him. It was precisely because he was loyal and loving that made her want to take that risk.

'I have the number of a local firm,' Moira

informed her with a pat on the arm Mae hoped was more out of friendship than pity.

'Okay, sweetheart, I'll just be downstairs if you need me.' Liam tucked Shannon under the covers and edged towards the door. She'd wanted to sleep in his bed, and after the night they'd had and the guilt he was still carrying he couldn't say no.

'I just have to make a phone call then I promise I'll be right up again.' He didn't want to leave her, even though he knew she was safe and would likely be asleep before he reached the bottom of the stairs. It had been a long night for everyone. But he had also promised to call Mae.

Although it was late—technically speaking, it was early morning, but since no one had slept he still counted it as night—he suspected Mae would be up. She'd been great tonight, helping with Shannon, and he was sure she'd want to be kept up to date with her progress. He'd already called his parents to let them know Shannon was fine, with no sign of concussion and a cast on her arm to show off in school that day. Their profuse apologies hadn't been necessary when it was his fault he'd left Shannon there, his only thoughts having been of the time he'd get to spend with Mae. He hoped his reassurances would help them get some sleep.

This call was going to be a little more difficult and painful. He'd waited until he'd come home to give him some space to think things over first, and to afford some privacy. Mae had been upfront about not wanting anything serious, so she deserved the same respect when it came to ending things.

She answered the call the second it rang. 'How is she?'

The concern in her voice made Liam ache all the more for the life he really wanted with Mae and Shannon. If only he could be sure that it would work between them, that she could commit to his family, he wouldn't have to choose between his daughter and her. It was a contest she could never win.

'They put a cast on her arm, but other than that she's fine. Currently asleep in my bed.

She's understandably clingy and didn't even want me to come down and phone you.'

'In that case, I won't keep you. I just wanted to know she was okay.' Mae was about to end the call but that wasn't what Liam wanted—none of this was. But, if he didn't have this conversation now, he'd have to do it at work and it wouldn't be fair to ambush her like that.

'Listen, Mae, tonight has really opened my eyes. I just don't think a casual fling is going to work for me...'

'I was thinking the same thing.'

Good, at least they were on the same page. It should make things easier if, as he thought, she'd realised the responsibility of looking after his daughter would be more commitment than she was ready to give.

'So, we'll just put this down to a lapse of judgement? A very, very nice one while it lasted, but I can't justify the time away from my daughter. I should have been with her tonight. She was looking for me when she fell, and I just can't let her down like that again. It's probably best we just go back to being work colleagues. I hope you understand.' It wouldn't do to beg her to consider something long term and more serious when he wasn't sure either of them could commit to that. He'd already messed up, and it had only been one day, so the damage he could manage to inflict on his relationship with his daughter was unimaginable and not worth the risk.

'Of course,' she said eventually, letting him breathe a sigh of relief.

'Okay, then… I guess I'll see you around.'

'I guess so.'

'Bye, Mae. I'm sorry things didn't work out.'

'Me too, Liam.' Her voice was quiet but she was the first to hang up.

Liam didn't have much practice at ending relationships; his last experience had been him on the other end of that conversation. It hadn't been his intention to cause Mae any pain, though she seemed to sympathise with the position he was in. He hadn't wanted her to get upset or feel rejected.

But, if he was honest, her stoic response stung. It was as if what they'd had together tonight didn't really matter. In other circumstances, he knew they could have had something really special, mostly because they already had. To find she was able to simply forget it so easily was not only a knock to his ego, but confirmation that she wasn't the one for him after all. If he was ever going to let someone back into his life permanently, it would have to be someone who would fight for them, who would show a commitment to Shannon and him that Mae obviously didn't want.

CHAPTER EIGHT

'AT LEAST YOU love me, Brodie, eh?' Mae cuddled her furry friend closely and shared her bag of crisps with him. Though he didn't seem interested in the soppy movie she'd selected for the evening's entertainment, he was enjoying the hugs and attention. It didn't even matter about the slobber and crumbs he'd got all over her leisure wear, as long as she had him to hug tonight instead of being completely on her own.

She'd substituted an Irish wolfhound for Liam: that was how great a hole had been left in her life in just a matter of days. It was her fault for breaking her own rules. No matter how short the fling, she apparently couldn't separate her emotions from a physical relationship. Although, sleeping with someone she would see on a regular basis had always been asking for trouble. Having dinner with his family and getting to know his daughter were extra red flags she'd chosen to ignore. Little wonder then that, when he prioritised Shannon's welfare over some fun with her, Mae had been bereft.

She had hoped they'd have a chance to explore their relationship a little more, but he'd made it clear he wasn't interested beyond the one night. At least she'd been able to walk away with her dignity intact, if not her heart. She'd known the score; it wasn't Liam's fault she couldn't control her emotions because she'd only gone and fallen for him.

In the short space of time she'd got to know him, she'd opened her heart and had been preparing to share a little bit more with him. He and Shannon had showed her what she was missing out on by shutting herself off from the possibility of love and family. She didn't feel any better now after a brief, albeit passionate, tryst with Liam than she had after a serious relationship with Diarmuid.

'Perhaps I should just give up on men altogether and become a dog lady,' she said to Brodie, who licked away her tears then snatched the last crisp out of her hand. Betrayed by another male.

For a little while she'd been able to believe that a future with someone was possible—a relationship, maybe even a family some day. Being dropped like a hot potato the second his daughter had needed him, though understandable, had been nonetheless crushing. It simply reiterated the notion that everyone left her eventually. Although, in this case it had happened pretty darn quick. Maybe this time she would learn her lesson and not give her heart to anyone again. She couldn't trust anyone with it, not even herself.

All the lies she'd told herself about not getting emotionally involved with Liam, knowing she liked him, had just been to cover the fact she wanted to be with him. Now here she was, crying and pouring her heart out to a dog, when her fling with Liam was supposed to have been just a bit of fun. Apparently, she wasn't capable of that without losing her heart and her mind over a man. Over Liam.

The tears started again and she buried her face in Brodie's fur, drawing some comfort from his warmth. It said a lot about her life that she was spending her evening with a dog because she was so lonely, a feeling that had only been exacerbated by having spent time with Liam and his family. She hadn't just lost him but Paddy, Moira and Shannon too. Once Ray was out of hospital, she wouldn't even have Brodie.

It would be easy to pack up and move on somewhere else where she wouldn't run the risk of seeing Liam again and endure the pain of knowing they couldn't be together. But she couldn't keep doing that after every failed romance. She wanted to settle down and be happy, even if that meant being on her own.

'You're very grumpy tonight, Daddy.' Shannon pouted at him.

'Am I? Sorry, sweetheart, I just have a lot on my mind.' Mostly a certain woman he couldn't stop thinking about.

It had been a couple of days since he'd ended things and, though it had ultimately been his decision, he missed Mae. It was funny how close they'd become in such a short space of time and how much impact she'd had on his family. His parents and Shannon had been asking after her ever since. He'd excused her absence as a clash of shifts but he couldn't use that line for ever. It was awkward when his mum and dad knew they'd slept together; that'd been obvious when they'd both arrived in the early hours after Shannon's accident. It was more difficult still when they knew he didn't just hook up with anyone.

No one since Clodagh, in fact. Mae was special, they all knew that, but they respected him enough to make his own mistakes and not throw it back in his face. He'd done enough self-flagellation about losing her to suffice. Although, he had noticed his mum phoning to check in with him more often, sending home-made comfort food with Shannon every day. As much as he was indulging heavily in the baked goods and carbs, none of it could replace the feel-good endorphins he'd only had when he'd been with Mae.

He was beginning to wonder if he'd jumped

the gun. If they might have been able to work something out that suited them both so he hadn't had to lose her altogether. She'd been quick to accept the end of their arrangement without quibble, so he supposed there was no compromise to be had. In hindsight, telling someone who'd been burned so badly in a relationship that he'd only accept a partner who'd be there for him and his daughter might have been overkill. Those high expectations were never going to be attainable after only one night together but it was too late now to go back.

Yes, he had regrets and, given some time to think things through more clearly, he would've done things differently. Right now, he'd do anything to have Mae back in his life in whatever capacity he could. She'd helped with Ray and Shannon, not to mention the fracas outside the pub. They'd worked as a team.

More than that, she'd been there for him when he'd needed it. Liam had found a peace with Mae that he hadn't had in a long time, and their short-lived fling had been the explosive candle on the cake. It was no wonder Shannon thought he was grumpy when he'd been mad at himself these past days for throwing all that away. They were both missing her, and ending things hadn't achieved anything in the long run when they were hurting anyway.

'I miss Mae too.' His daughter was more astute than he gave her credit for, though he didn't want to get into a conversation about why Mae was no longer in the picture. Shannon was too young to fully understand the intricacies of adult relationships. Apparently, so was he. He was still trying to understand his own actions and could only think that his knee-jerk reaction in ending things with Mae had been his defences kicking in. When Shannon had been hurt, that was all he'd been able to think of, and how he was to blame. It was something he was too used to doing since Clodagh had left him doing the sole parenting, but he realised now, too late, that he was entitled to live a life of his own, just like Shannon's mother.

'We're both busy people. You're my main

girl, Shannon, and don't you forget it.' He put an arm around her shoulders and gave her a squeeze before opening the back door. It was then he realised he must have left it unlocked after their last visit. Thankfully, Brodie made an excellent burglar deterrent, and he would have heard him bark if a stranger had attempted to get in.

Shannon shrugged him off. 'Da-ad. I'm not going to be a kid for ever, you know. You really do need to get yourself a life.'

She flounced off into Ray's house, giving him a glimpse of the teenage years yet to come, and he knew she was right. Some day she wasn't going to want him anywhere near her and then where would he be? Likely sitting drowning his sorrows in his parents' place, lamenting a lost love that he let get away.

'You're such an eejit,' he chastised himself, only for his daughter's squeal coming from the living room to make him forget all his recent bad decisions for a moment.

'Shannon? What's wrong?' He burst through

the door, half-expecting to see her lying hurt somewhere.

Instead, he was met with the sight of her hugging Mae, with Brodie jumping on both of them, trying to be a part of the happy reunion.

'Hey,' Mae said quietly when she spotted him, furtively glancing around the living room, as if he'd caught her doing something she shouldn't. There was an empty family-sized bag of crisps lying on the sofa in between the pile of cushions, her shoes had been kicked off onto the floor and the credits of a movie were playing on the TV. She'd obviously been here for a while. If he'd known that, he might have come over earlier.

'Hey. Sorry. I didn't think you'd still be coming over to see to Brodie.' He had assumed she would have ditched the dog-sitting, in an attempt to avoid him, when it was as much a favour to him as to Ray.

'Of course I would. I promised Ray. I wouldn't leave Brodie on his own simply because we'd agreed not to see each other.' She frowned at him and he realised immediately what an injustice he'd done even to think that of her. Mae would never have purposely left anyone in the lurch. She was too good a person. Perhaps deep down he'd known that and had come over tonight because there was a chance of running into her like this.

'Did you and Daddy fall out? Is that why you've been crying, Mae?' Shannon asked, eyeballing the two of them before Liam had a chance to apologise to Mae for underestimating her.

'I haven't—'

'That's adult business.' He managed to talk over Mae in his lame attempt to distract his daughter. 'Sorry, I didn't mean to interrupt.'

'I was just saying I haven't been crying. It, er, must be my allergies.'

'What did you do, Daddy?' Shannon, not fooled by either of them, was fairly and correctly putting the blame on his shoulders for any upset Mae had suffered.

Now that Shannon had pointed it out, he could see the red rings around Mae's usually bright and clear green eyes, and she didn't look at all like her normal glam self. She was wearing pale-pink sweatpants and a matching baggy sweater, without a trace of make-up on her face. Whilst he still thought her beautiful, it was apparent that she hadn't put in her usual effort with her appearance.

He was guilty of the same tonight, dressing for comfort rather than style because it didn't seem important. Nothing did against the ache in his heart, which had been growing stronger since the last time he'd seen Mae. He almost hoped that her casual attire was an outward reflection of her heartache too, so that he knew he'd meant more to her than a one-night stand.

'He didn't do anything, Shannon. Your daddy just wants to spend all the time he can with you.' Mae stepped in to save his blushes, as his daughter was probably gearing up to give him a stern telling off.

'I see him every day,' Shannon said, rolling her eyes to make them both laugh. There he was, trying to be present in her life, when it seemed as though he was nothing but a nuisance. Perhaps he should let Shannon make all the important decisions in their lives from now on. She certainly wouldn't have let Mae walk away so easily.

'That's because he's a very good dad. I haven't seen my father since I was a little girl. You're very lucky you have someone so lovely taking care of you.' Mae was fixing Shannon's braid over her shoulder and Liam knew she was feeling the loss of her mother all over again. She was someone who should never have been on her own when she had so much love to give. It was clear in the way she was with Shannon, so loving and tender, that she would have made a great mum. If only men like him had treated her better, she might have believed it too.

'Did your daddy go away, like my mummy?'

'Yes, he did, but aren't you lucky you still get to see your mummy?'

The hitch in Mae's voice hinted at the pain she was still going through at the loss of her own mother, something he thankfully had no experience of, but sympathised with. After all, he'd fallen apart when a loved one had simply moved out of the house and the relationship; he could only imagine losing someone for ever. He had spent these past days thinking of nothing else and he knew he couldn't waste the second chance he'd been given. Opportunities to reconnect didn't come around often and he didn't want to spend the rest of his life hating himself for not grabbing it with both hands.

'Not every day, but I see daddy all the time when he's not at work.' Blissfully oblivious to Mae's distress, Shannon was very philosophical about her circumstances, showing just how much she'd adapted to the new dynamic already. Better than her father, it seemed.

'That's what makes him such a good daddy. He wants to be there for you all the time so you never, ever get hurt again.' Mae gently touched the cast on Shannon's arm, and Liam got the impression she felt as guilty that it had happened as he did.

It occurred to him that accepting responsibility for an accident that had been beyond her control was ridiculous, yet that was exactly what he'd done. He'd blamed himself for something he could never have prevented, to the extent he'd thought he had to stay glued to his daughter's side—a notion she clearly wasn't a fan of and, now he could see the situation from a different point of view, something completely unnecessary.

'That's just silly. He's not with me when I'm at school, or asleep.' She had a point. There was nothing to say she wouldn't fall or have an accident when he was at work or in a different room. He couldn't be in two different places at once and it was stupid to think otherwise. It was time he stopped using his daughter as an excuse to keep Mae at a distance and make that leap of faith.

'Shannon, could you go into the kitchen and give Brodie some water? I'd like to talk to Mae.' He wanted a little privacy so he didn't embarrass Mae, or himself, if she wasn't interested in anything more between them, and if he'd imagined the lingering embers of their passion still glowing, waiting to be stoked once more.

Shannon skipped off with Brodie galloping behind her. Mae faced him, her arms wrapped around her body, hugging herself in an expression of self-defence and anxiety.

She wasn't the same spiky American he'd sparred with during their first meeting. Although she'd let down those protective barriers and let him in, he'd wounded her with his actions, and he was sorry for that.

'Sorry. I wasn't expecting anyone over. Ray will probably be home tomorrow, so I was just saying my goodbyes to Brodie. I'll tidy up before I leave.' She glanced around at the evidence of her pity party. Liam recognised the signs, since he'd left a similar scene behind at home—his wallowing illustrated by chocolate wrappers and empty coffee cups.

He shook his head. 'That's not what I wanted to talk to you about. I, er, I missed you.'

She gave him a half-smile which he wasn't sure came from pity or something else. 'I missed you too.'

He wanted to say more, but instead he gathered her into his arms and held her tight. He felt huge relief when she wrapped her arms around him in response, instead of recoiling or pushing him away, which she would have had every right to do.

Eventually Mae let go. 'How's Shannon? She seems okay. No permanent psychological damage?'

He could tell by the way she was biting her lip that she was teasing him.

'Okay, so I was being a little bit over-protective and a tad over the top.'

'Just a tad. But I understand why. She's your daughter. You feel responsible, and you're afraid that she'll get hurt because of your actions.'

'Exactly.' And Mae's grasp of his situation, her empathy, was why he wanted to fight for her.

'I would never want her to get hurt either. You have to do what's best.'

'Yes…yes, I do. For once, I want to do whatever's best for me, and I think that's to have you back in my life. I know you don't want anything serious, Mae, but do you think we could still see each other? You know, maybe go out every now and then?' It wouldn't be the instant happy family he'd dreamed of, but he was willing to take things slowly if it meant he would still have Mae around.

'With Shannon?'

'Not if you don't want that…' He didn't want to frighten her off if she was even considering forgiving him and wanting to try again.

'I think maybe it's time we both stopped being afraid of being with each other. We can't hide away for ever, living in fear that we'll get hurt again, and letting the good things slip away from us. We're good together.' She slid her arms back around his waist, that connection making him remember their night together, and promising the thrill of more.

'That we are. So… I can stop pretending to Shannon and my parents that we're only colleagues?' If Mae was willing to try again, it seemed plausible that they should be open about it this time.

She cocked her head to one side. 'You really think we ever had them fooled?'

He thought about it for a split second. 'Nah. I think they knew before we even did.'

'We better prepare ourselves for the "we told you so" conversation.'

'It's fine. I can handle it. It's better than the, "you eejit, why did you let her go?" one I've been having with myself.'

'You are an eejit, but you're my eejit.' Mae tilted her face up to his and sealed their new beginning with a tender kiss.

'Always,' he replied, knowing he'd found the woman he'd been missing in his life long before they'd even known each other. It had taken them some time to work out that they were meant to be together but, now they had, Liam would do everything it took to make the relationship work.

He and Mae had finally found in one another the family they'd both been searching for.

EPILOGUE

'SHANNON, DON'T GO too far. Stay where we can see you!' Mae shouted after the little girl as she ran ahead into the woods.

'As if we could miss that dog, and since it's glued to her side there isn't much chance of losing either of them. It gives us a few minutes' peace, at least. Maybe even time to make out.' Liam nuzzled into her neck, his warm breath on her skin already making her wish they hadn't got out of bed this morning.

They'd only been together six months, but it was enough time for both of them to know it was what they both wanted and needed. She'd moved in with Liam and Shannon after a few weeks of dating, neither of them having wanted to waste any time that could've been spent together. It made practical sense too, making sure there was usually someone at home for Shannon, and saving on the travelling. On the odd occasion they were both working, Paddy and Moira were only too happy to babysit. Mae felt as though she was part of a real family now. Especially on those Sunday afternoons when Liam's parents cooked them a roast dinner that couldn't be beaten.

They'd even got the dog to complete the family picture. Technically he was still Ray's but it had made sense for them to take Brodie on a more permanent basis while Ray was working to overcome his alcohol issue. Ray was attending support meetings, and stopping drinking had definitely improved his health. Although his condition was irreversible, abstaining from alcohol would give him a longer life expectancy than if he'd continued to drink. He'd even put on a little weight since he'd started eating better, aided by the home-cooked meals Liam's parents sent round for him. Mae and Liam had him round for dinner every now and then to check in with him and give him some company.

Ray kept Brodie with him during the day, but mostly it was down to Liam and Mae to feed and walk the wolfhound. Shannon was absolutely besotted with the mutt, and Mae was sure he had helped her adjust to the upheaval when she'd moved in. She still saw her mother on occasion, which gave Mae and Liam some alone time.

They were very much still in the honeymoon stage, but the way he made her melt every time he touched her convinced her it would always be the same for them. In and out of the bedroom they made a good team, and she was thankful that both she and Liam had taken that leap of faith in one another to try and make things work.

'Not the kissing *again*.' Shannon voiced her disgust at the kissing they'd progressed to, so engrossed in one another, they hadn't heard her come back.

In typical Liam style, he responded by planting a smacker on his daughter's cheek. 'I wouldn't want you to feel left out. You're still my number one girl.'

'Ew!' Shannon wiped away all trace of him

with the back of her hand. 'Can we go and have dinner now, Daddy? You said we could go out to celebrate.'

'Oh? That's the first I've heard.' Mae turned to Liam, wondering what they were celebrating, other than having an afternoon off together.

Out of the corner of her eye she saw him gesturing to Shannon to zip her lips. He was always surprising her with romantic meals or movie nights, working hard to ensure they weren't just parenting Shannon together but constantly investing in their relationship. She appreciated that, along with the daily conversations that kept them a part of each other's lives even during those busier times. He was doing everything to make sure this relationship worked and keep her happy, though he only had to be in her orbit to do that. She'd never felt so safe and loved.

'I have something for you. Or, rather, Brodie does. Come here, boy!' He called the dog, which bounded over, and on Liam's direction jumped up on Mae, his front paws resting on her shoulders.

'What is it?' She was too busy fending off Brodie's kisses and trying to keep her balance to understand what was going on.

'On his collar.'

There, attached to Brodie's name tag, was a beautiful diamond ring. She looked at Liam, her mouth open, eyes wide, afraid to believe what was happening. When he knelt down in the pile of leaves on the ground and took her hand, she just about stopped breathing.

'Mae Watters, I know we haven't been together long, but this feels too right not to act on it. Will you please be my wife and make our little family complete?'

It was all too much, and she felt the tears pricking the back of her eyes at the pure love for her this man emanated. Even Shannon was clapping beside him, apparently in on this plot and accepting it, which was much more important. They hadn't discussed marriage. After Diarmuid and her last doomed wedding day, she hadn't thought she'd ever want to make that level of commitment again. But these past months with Liam and Shannon had been the happiest of her life, and she was ready for more. Ready to commit herself to this family.

'Yes! Yes, I will, Liam O'Conner.' She held out her hand whilst he wrestled the ring off the dog to place it on her finger. 'I guess you were pretty confident I was going to say yes if you already planned a celebratory dinner?'

'If that didn't work, I was hoping I could kiss you into submission.'

This time Shannon cheered when they kissed, and they didn't care who was watching.

Mae couldn't help but think her mum would be proud she'd discovered her Irish roots after all.

* * * * *

If you enjoyed this story, check out these other great reads from Karin Baine

Surgeon Prince's Fake Fiancée
A Mother for His Little Princess
Nurse's Risk with the Rebel
Falling Again for the Surgeon

All available now!